TRUST ON LIFE SUPPORT

A NOVEL ABOUT
THE LIFE OF A FEMALE
CORRECTIONS OFFICER

AJUT

 iUniverse®

TRUST ON LIFE SUPPORT
A NOVEL ABOUT THE LIFE OF A FEMALE
CORRECTIONS OFFICER

Copyright © 2017 Ajut.

Inspired by actual events.
This is a work of fiction. Names, characters, places, and incidents are either the product of the author's imagination or used fictitiously, and any resemblance to actual persons-living or dead-events, or locales is entirely coincidental.

iUniverse books may be ordered through booksellers or by contacting:

iUniverse
1663 Liberty Drive
Bloomington, IN 47403
www.iuniverse.com
1-800-Authors (1-800-288-4677)

Because of the dynamic nature of the Internet, any web addresses or links contained in this book may have changed since publication and may no longer be valid. The views expressed in this work are solely those of the author and do not necessarily reflect the views of the publisher, and the publisher hereby disclaims any responsibility for them.

Any people depicted in stock imagery provided by Getty Images are models, and such images are being used for illustrative purposes only.
Certain stock imagery © Getty Images.

ISBN: 978-1-5320-4338-3 (sc)
ISBN: 978-1-5320-4340-6 (hc)
ISBN: 978-1-5320-4339-0 (e)

Library of Congress Control Number: 2018904190

Print information available on the last page.

iUniverse rev. date: 04/102018

DEDICATION WITH GRATITUDE

To the memory of my Husband until death did we part, was on Life Support when he eventually passed away from cancer before I could finish my book. Even through his pain and suffering he was determined to make me or anyone in his presence smile or laugh. To my mother, the matriarch of my family. She is the rock of stability from which I stand, the life and air that I breathe, without her there would be no me. To my late Aunt, who taught me to be self-confident, no matter the circumstance. To my late grandmother for her steadfast dignity and prayer. To my children for their patience and confidence. To my grandchildren, my entire family and friends for their ongoing support and immense love. Lastly, to my late father, who for me, embodied metaphorically the term, Trust on Life Support. Being the mentally unstable human being that he was, left me no choice, but to trust that he would not cause a fatal accidental due to his violent behavior. Hence, Trust on Life Support. Most of all, I am grateful to the almighty for the opportunity to travel this magnificent journey of life.

UTOPIA

THE WORD REFERS TO AN ideal place or state of mind where everyone lives in harmony. Everything is for the best, and everything is perfect. My father gave me the nickname Utopia, and he was the only one allowed to use it.

Correction vs. Corruption
Officer vs. Prisoner
Officer vs. Officer
Prisoner vs. Prisoner

There is no mercy among the prisoners. There is no honor among the officers. Both are institutionalized and locked down. Both wear uniforms, abide by the rules, eat the same food, use the same bathrooms, have state numbers, wear ID badges, and rat each other out. Officers murder officers, prisoners murder prisoners, and each murders the other. Both serve time to the tune of a retirement date, a release date, or ultimately death. Lastly, each group has a high rate of suicide—one more so than the other, and that is of the officers.

THE LAW OF SURVIVAL
SLIPPIN' INTO DARKNESS

I MAINTAINED MY CORRECTIONS OFFICER position until retirement, all the while clutching onto my sanity as I watched the psyches of my fellow officers go from sane to insane. One of the most unscrupulous things in law enforcement is a corrupt officer. In fact, it might be the very worst thing. Lord knows I fought hard against becoming institutionalized. Perhaps it was the feeling of being held captive behind those massive concrete walls and barbed wire fences that drove many to snap. It is certainly difficult for any individual to be locked up inside a maximum security state prison, day after day and year after year. The sense of enclosure that comes from confinement will eventually take its toll on even the strongest human being, a toll that can have everlasting effects. I have to say, without a doubt, that it definitely took its toll on me.

Over time, my training and experience became increasingly insignificant. Prison life has to be one of the lowest points in anyone's life. I experienced intense pressure that became so all-consuming that I came to fear, above all else, that I would be the next officer to lose her mind or self-control. Sensing that officers were losing touch with reality was unnerving. It was bad enough dealing with the prisoners' disconnect from reality. But as time progressed, I learned more and more to trust my instincts and stand firm, without compromise, on my own principles and values, which stemmed from my father's teachings about men and how I could anticipate they'd behave toward women.

What was most discouraging was having to accept the fact that it was becoming more and more difficult to view the officer and the prisoner as two different kinds of individuals. The anxiety mounted, and eventually my state of mind was one of constant fear, accompanied by an urgent desire to escape the entrapment of prison. I just wanted to go home, where I felt safe and secure. My drive to the prison was like driving into a recurring nightmare, and my drive home was like a great escape from hell. I could feel my soul slipping into darkness. I swear—I did not want to be the next officer leaving in a straitjacket, handcuffs, or, even worse, a body bag. I prayed daily that I wouldn't be next, because I didn't know whether it would be me; after all, who was I not to be next?

Who knows the defining moment when one slips into insanity? What I was seeing just did not make any sense. Why were officers of the law stepping over the line, right into the line of fire, without any misgivings? That was my question then—and now. When does someone make the decision to give up on oneself or turn one's back on oneself? Suicides were mounting, on both sides of the wall, by both officers and prisoners.

These are the unrelenting facets of *Trust on Life Support*. And the games that were sexual in nature were just a minuscule part of the sinister pastimes that permeated the prison. The prisoner has nothing better to do and all day to do it. The mind games, or brainwashing, are things all corrections officers should learn to recognize and be prepared for, as prisoners and corrupt officers will try to dupe them. I was somewhat fortunate in that respect, as I could recognize that mentality because many of the same games are played in the streets of the inner cities, and prison culture is pretty much like the hard-core streets where I grew up and lived throughout my life. Therefore, when I arrived for duty and entered the gates of hell, I'd already learned to be conscious of the kind of place I was entering. As a result, I assumed the mind-set of the law of the streets, which is the law of survival.

PREFACE

I CAME TO AN EPIPHANY one morning while standing post, watching the prisoners do what they did best on visit day: unraveling the female's psyche in the worst way. I remember asking myself, "Why am I just standing here watching this miserable process of human degradation? I am just standing here doing nothing." In any case, there was nothing that I could do to change the situation or the miserable conditions. "There has to be a reason I'm here, other than the salary." That's when it hit me. *The outside world should know what's going on in this inside world.* "Perhaps I'm here to tell the story." The only way I could shed some light on the dreadful conditions that lie within these concrete walls was to write a book. As a woman and a victim of domestic violence, I wanted to zero in on the misogyny and the sexual objectification that was going on behind the wall.

Once I started thinking and then writing, I found that I was telling my own story. It took me back to my life of turmoil and domestic violence that had begun with the abuse of my mother at the hands of my father. Not only was I opening up about my personal abuse, but I also started remembering all sorts of stories about the women in my realm, my family and my friends. Now, here I was dealing with the abuse of female visitors and female prisoners. This epiphany opened up an area in my mind and in my life that I had intentionally flung to the side. Well, maybe I should rephrase that—an area in my mind I had suppressed. The more I wrote, the more I allowed the memories to flow without trying to bottle them up again. I found myself consoling the abused women who visited the jail, as well as the female prisoners, regarding their abusive relationships, whether it was with a male or female, and even the abuse from the male officers. Sometimes lending a caring ear—not saying anything, just listening—is all that is needed to help someone make a move for help. However, when I did stumble upon a threatening situation, I would assist in any area that was possible. I only shared my abusive, violent experiences when I thought it would alleviate the pain of another victim.

When I began working inside the prisons, my conversations regarding domestic violence became more and more frequent. That one day, in particular, brought me to an even deeper awareness— that perhaps I could not only write about the horrific conditions on the inside and shed some light on the prison environment, but I could also help women and young girls from all walks of life who are victims of abuse to see themselves clearly and to eventually seek help some way, somehow. I believe we are reflections of one another.

INTRODUCTION

MOST PRISON STORIES ARE TOLD by men, about men, whether it's an officer or a prisoner. My experience as a female corrections officer in a maximum security state prison for men offers a distinct perspective. These are some of my personal experiences. Also, I will share my experiences about a state correctional facility for women and the differences between the prisons and the male and female prisoners. I believe the public, in general, is intrigued about the mysteries behind the huge concrete walls. Most people don't have a clue about what goes on inside these massive prisons, unless they have been a resident—an officer or a prisoner. Even those who visit on a regular basis don't really know what happens on the inside. They merely come and go, never going inside, only visiting on the borders of the prison.

It's unfortunate that many of these visitors, particularly

females, are a major contributing factor to the travesties that exist behind the wall. State prisons are cesspools with no moral compass. It's much like quicksand, easy to get sucked in and hard to get out, especially for those who think they can dabble with the criminal mind. They are the ones who sink further and further until they become completely submerged into the abyss of the prison's bottomless pit. Female visitors and children especially are calculated prey and become emotionally and psychologically trapped in this secluded world of coldhearted criminals, misogyny, and sexual objectification, manipulated by love. It's almost as if the women become spellbound or hypnotized, and there seems to be nothing that can break the spell or the hypnosis.

It doesn't matter who she is or why she has dared to enter their territory. The prisoners control it; it's their domain. Nevertheless, she enters from all walks of life—officers, attorneys, nurses, educators, even, religious volunteers. Furthermore, if she believes for an instant that she can play the game with a criminal mind or thinks that she can't be duped, it is at that very instant that she becomes powerless to her own thoughts and then, her own actions. Consequently, she subjects herself to the criminal suggestion and behavior that gives way to corruption, domestic violence, sexism, rape, child abuse, drug and sex trafficking, and the list goes on. Although I was a victim of domestic violence myself, my encounters don't hold a candle to what I've witnessed behind the gates of hell. What's more is that, the other men on the inside—that is, the male officers—are just as bad as, or worse than, the male prisoners, seeing as they are sometimes pitted against the females in collusion with the prisoners. Therefore, it is indisputably a man's world were a female should always be in the mind frame of what I consider to be "trust on life support" since her trust could very well cause her to lose her life.

A FEMALE CORRECTIONS OFFICER

TO BECOME A CORRECTIONS OFFICER and work behind the wall of a maximum male security prison is grueling, especially for a female, because she can be lulled into a false sense of security and become swayed by the flattering remarks of both the male prisoners and the male officers. This is somewhat like the calm before the storm. In my narrative about my personal experiences as a female corrections officer, you will discover, as I did, that the men are one and the same. In truth, my peers were just as corrupt as the convicted felons—and even more so in terms of trying to invade the female's psyche and rob her of her worthiness. Over time I was no longer concerned about the convicted criminal, the prisoner; I had to protect myself from the criminal who was not yet convicted: the officer.

To my dismay, I am being brutally honest. A large number of the male officers were exceptionally blatant in this regard. They had a strange sense of entitlement due to the fact that they were our colleagues, not prisoners. Convinced of this idiotic line of reasoning, they were brazen and unashamed of their indecent proposals and propositions, not to mention their deceptive practices. The male prisoners and officers both were flagrant in their attempts to violate the female's sense of self-worth. Listen, the bottom line is that behind the wall, it's a man's world. In this world, there is a relentless competition going on over who will be the first to break her *in*, or break her *down*. The only differences between these two men are the colors of their uniforms.

THE PRESENCE OF A WOMAN

IN THE BEGINNING, SHE IS identified as fresh new meat. Her mere presence and natural scent is extraordinarily evocative to the prisoners. I believe that a woman's scent is as powerful as the scent of one animal to another in the wild. When the opposite sex enters the clutches of the men behind the wall, where the overall majority are sexually deprived, the entire atmosphere of the prison changes simply because of her nearness. Her presence is so powerful that merely knowing there is a new female (fresh new meat) in the midst causes unrest among the men, both prisoners and officers, with their animalistic instincts.

This is the onset of their competitions and mind games. As it's been said, "Let the games begin!" It's nothing but child's play for a prisoner to find out whether or not the female can be intimidated or manipulated. Simply by making eye contact, he can catch the fear in her eyes. If she wears her heart in her panties, she easily could be persuaded to engage in illicit sex, which, again, is the beginning of the end. Although male officers engage in sexual misconduct and are lured into the mind games as well, their involvement in such activities cannot be considered equivalent to the female officer's sexual involvement because if a prisoner impregnates her, this takes the situation to the point of no return.

This is an ongoing fact that cannot be overemphasized. Any female who takes on the position of a corrections officer should understand the power of her presence and use it wisely, or it will unequivocally be used against her for a price, a price that will lead to a string of irreversible consequences. She should understand that she has everything to lose with nothing to gain, while the prisoner has everything to gain with nothing to lose. We all know that when fresh meat goes bad, new fresh meat is required.

ENTER AT YOUR OWN RISK: DANGER ZONE

AFTER MANY YEARS OF EXPERIENCE working behind the wall, these are my personal words of warning to those of you who dare to become a corrections officer, especially if you are a woman. You must realize that you will be locked up with the worst-of-the-worst men behind a ten-foot concrete wall, completely surrounded by razor wire fencing from top to bottom. Keep in mind that you will be totally alienated from the outside world, unable to leave until someone with a key allows you to exit. Therefore, I suggest you take a moment to say a prayer for your safety as soon as you make that conscious decision to enter the lion's den and become prey for the predators. In the meantime, the predators will prepare to compete against one another to see who is going to devour you first.

The hard-core reality is that this is a distinct world, cut off from your world and regulated by the prisoners and the laws of the streets. Therefore, a little bit of street smarts will go a long way, so get to know their lingo. For one, CYA is the acronym for "cover your ass." This code is strongly enforced among prisoners and officers.

If you were under the assumption that the prisoners are handcuffed at all times, you are in for a rude awakening. This is their world where they are allowed to roam freely, and 99 percent of the time, they are unrestrained, and you are unarmed. Unlike police officers on the streets, who carry their firearms 24-7, 365 days of the year, behind the wall some corrections officers are only permitted to carry a stick, which is referred to as a baton. Corrections officers can choose to purchase a firearm after being employed for one year. When reporting to the prison for duty, however, they must relinquish their personal firearm to the armory, which is located *outside* of the prison. Corrections officers are only permitted to carry that weapon *outside* of the prison while *off* duty.

Under certain circumstances they will be issued a departmental firearm by the state, for example, when transporting prisoners to and from a courthouse, hospital, police department or another prison. These same firearms are assigned for specific posts on the *outside* perimeters of the prison, such as the towers, or during a riot, a lockdown, or an escape, providing there are enough weapons to go around. These are also the few times that the prisoner will be handcuffed and, on occasion, shackled.

By the way, so you won't be surprised, many inmates do not like to be referred to as an inmate. Most often they will insist that you refer to them as prisoners. Their peculiar logic behind this request is "prisoners are held against their will." They believe they are being held against their will, regardless of the fact that they have been tried and convicted, and are presently serving time in prison. This is just a sneak peek at of some of their psyche.

My personal approach was to address prisoners with the utmost respect, irrespective of their convictions. Therefore, I insisted that the respect be reciprocated. This was essential for me as an officer and a woman. I believe that no one man is more deserving than another. I wasn't there to judge. I addressed them by their surname, preceded by "mister," and never by their first name. You will notice officers and prisoners addressing one another by their first names. The prisoners are not your friends; never give them that impression.

Overall, it is of the utmost importance that you first respect yourself, and then respect for you most often will follow, but not all of the time. Keep in mind that an officer's respect and reputation carries credence much greater than their badge and uniform. Please take heed to what I am saying. One mistake behind the wall can cause you to lose your freedom as well. Sadly, you will witness this happening among your fellow officers far too often. Nevertheless, the facts are obvious. You will be comingling with the criminally insane and convicted criminals on a daily basis. Occasionally, you will be with them more than you will be at home with your family. Please be mindful, without cease, that the prison belongs to the prisoners, and they are in complete control at all times. Always be conscious that they have the ability to take over the prison at any given time, rendering you powerless and vulnerable. From that point, you are a hostage subjected to being brutally tortured, repeatedly raped, beaten, and ultimately killed.

These thoughts should be a requisite for your survival and should run through your mind continuously to keep yourself in check and, most of all, to stay alive. Remember: you are always outnumbered! There is never room for error. To that end, if you have the preconceived notion that because you are a female and have certain assets—a pretty face, a voluptuous body, or any other tangible pleasures that are pleasing to a man—and you believe these assets make you less of a prey, then you are truly naive. As a matter of fact, those assets make you even more of a prey.

The objective for the *men* on the *inside*, and I am referring to prisoners and officers, is to swindle the female into becoming a useful tool—a trafficker of all sorts of contraband—as soon as she sells her soul. While this can be an ongoing challenge among the men, at other times, they work in cahoots with one another. We all know a prisoner's resources are limited; therefore, outside connections are a necessity, and that's where you or any other naive officer comes into play. Metaphorically speaking, you must look at this environment as if it is a lion's den—that is, kill or be killed. It is solely about *your* survival because once they have invaded your mind, you have lost all control. Any control that you thought you had is destined for disaster.

I do not know how to make this any clearer. The prisoners do not give a *fuck* about you! They have nothing to lose. You, on the other hand, will lose your respect, your dignity, and possibly your freedom or your life. Bartering with a prisoner is like eating a slice of the devil's pie. If you ever put yourself in this precarious position, you have undoubtedly reached the point of no return. Please be attentive to yourself, and remember, that your intuition is your best friend. Consequently, when you feel something is not right, take heed and be prepared for the deadly mind games that are materializing. If you are not focused on your surroundings at all times and allow deception to creep in, you are not only detrimental to yourself, but you also have become a threat to the entire institution. Prisoners have already forfeited their freedom; don't forfeit yours.

Last but not least, I am sorry to say, I have witnessed firsthand many officers being led out in handcuffs and returning as prisoners, and that's if they don't go out in a body bag or are found dead on the streets. Please make every effort never to become lackadaisical. Many officers have lost their lives, not only at the hands of prisoners, but also at the hands of each other because of their deceitful games. For the record, the suicide rate among corrections officers is much greater than that of the prisoners. Let me finish by saying, you definitely have to have the courage to willfully walk into a danger zone without protection. So, beware. You are entering at your own risk.

PRISON VS. GHETTO

THE ATMOSPHERE OF THE INSIDE of a prison is extremely similar to the atmosphere of the ghetto. This was undeniably advantageous for me during my career as a corrections officer because I was raised in the inner-city housing projects. This experience coupled with my personal misfortunes certainly prepared me for the rough environment behind the walls of the prisons. Mayhem is an ongoing process in the prisons as it is in the streets of the ghetto. For instance, in my young adult life, I was a victim of an armed robbery, a purse snatching, and a carjacking, all in broad daylight. In addition, I was a victim of domestic violence during my childhood, a witness to the violence between my parents, and later a victim of physical abuse in my own marriage, which ended acrimoniously. This is not to say, in any way, form, or fashion, that domestic violence primarily exists in rough neighborhoods. I am simply pointing out ways that I have been criminally victimized and violated.

Eventually, my misfortunes throughout my upbringing allowed me to identify with the rough edges of prison, such as the lingo and the grittiness of it all. In the long run, it enabled me to demonstrate unyielding courage, a characteristic that was imperative while "serving my time" as an officer. I allude to my tenure as serving time because the more you read, the more you will see the similarities between officers and prisoners, with respect to their incarceration and restrictions. In comparing the aspect of serving time, for example, the corrections officer is only allowed to go home at night, and that's only if there isn't a lockdown in progress. Otherwise, both are locked up; neither one is allowed to leave until the officer's shift or the prisoner's sentence ends—unless the officer resigns or retires.

While growing up in the inner city, I became attuned to living among criminals, gangbangers, pimps, prostitutes, junkies, and drug dealers. The same pungent smell of alcohol, drugs, and filth that reeked throughout the streets of the ghetto also reeked throughout the prisons. It was a daily routine for me to literally step over and around liquor bottles, drug vials, and hypodermic needles while walking through the neighborhoods and the dilapidated hallways of the projects—not to mention running up on a dead corpse every now and again. I learned how to tread through the streets as if I owned everything in sight, similar to the way a lion treads through the jungle—fearless.

I treaded through the prison in the same manner, moving as fast as I could, and never wasting time or hanging around. Where I come from, I was taught that idle time breeds trouble. It is the same concept behind the wall: "stick and move," in other words, do what you have to do and keep it moving. Needless to say, the derelicts and drug dealers in the inner city considered the hallways and doorways of the projects their haven, making it a daily task for residents to enter and exit—not only the buildings but also their own apartments. At times the prisoners were allowed to hang out as well. For these reasons, I would pray every day for my safety, just as I did each day before reporting for duty at to lineup. This was a way of life for me growing up in the ghetto, and ironically, upon becoming a corrections officer, that way of life came into existence again.

HURT TO LOVE HIM,
HURT TO HATE HIM

I HAD TO BE ABOUT two years old when my father picked me up and placed my little body on top of a bedroom dresser. I was so small that I vividly remember seeing my entire body in the dresser's mirror as I stood there staring at myself. My father placed me on top of the dresser so I would not be in his way while he physically abused my mother. We were staying in a one-room flat the size of a small bedroom, equipped with a toilet, sink, bed, and dresser. Oblivious to what was about to happen, I was gazing at myself in the mirror when suddenly I saw my father slapping and punching my mother around the room as if she was a rag doll. All I could do was watch helplessly.

After beating her senseless, he had the audacity to demand that she stop crying and go wash her teary eyes and bloody face.

She hurried over to a small sink attached to the wall outside of the bathroom to do what he ordered. Then he stormed into the bathroom, slamming the door behind him. My mother immediately grabbed me. While trying to control her sobbing, she assured me that everything was going to be fine. This was the first of countless abusive episodes between my parents that I would witness throughout my life. From there, I remember moving to a couple of different places and eventually into a spacious one-bedroom apartment. What stood out to me the most was the shiny, immaculate linoleum on the floors.

Late one night, shortly after moving in, I remember awakening to the quiet tone of my mother's voice. "Get up, baby, and come with me," she said. "We have to leave right away." The apartment was filled with a light gray film of smoke; however, I didn't know what that was at the time. "Where are we going?" I asked. As she slipped an orange-flavored baby aspirin into my mouth, she responded, "Just listen to what I tell you to do. We have to leave right now." Then she snugly wrapped me, pajamas and all, into my blanket and lifted me into her arms. In hindsight, she was noticeably calm.

The next thing I remember, we were standing in front of the living room window and looking down at a crowd of people, who were looking up at us. In the middle of the crowd, I saw flashing red lights emanating from the vehicles of police officers and firefighters. It seemed as though there were hundreds of them. My next recollection was peculiar: I was on the street with the same crowd of people in the arms of a firefighter. I was wondering where my mother was when I heard my father yelling for both of us. When I looked around, I could see that he was pushing his way through the crowd but was instantly handcuffed and placed into the back of a police cruiser. He was intoxicated. I could tell by the rage in his voice and his violent behavior.

Through all of this, I still didn't know what was going on. Everything was happening so fast, it was like going through a whirlwind from the moment my mother had awakened me. And when I did see my father, I thought he was going through another one of his rages in an attempt to attack my mother. At any rate, I was relieved that the police officers stopped him dead in his tracks. Then I remember being awakened by my aunt's soft voice. "Are you all right, baby?" When I opened my eyes, I saw my mother for the first time since she'd had me in her arms and we were standing in front of the window looking down into the crowd of people. At this point, we were in my aunt's home with a host of other relatives, who were asking all sorts of questions about what had happened the night before.

While my aunt was comforting me, I could hear my mother giving the details about the succession of events. She said, "Last night, early in the evening, there was a fight between two men in the building. Later that night, one of them returned with a Molotov cocktail bomb, threw it into the stairwell of the building, and ignited a fire on the first floor." When my mother did wake me, the first floor of the building was completely engulfed in flames, and we were trapped on the third floor, which was also the top floor. Then I learned why we were standing in front of the window. She described how she secured my body in a blanket, covering my face, and dropped me into a fire safety net, and she followed. Apparently, the building didn't have a fire escape. The only thing I remembered was being held in the arms of a firefighter when, out of nowhere, I heard and saw my father in one of his usual rampages.

Soon thereafter, the Salvation Army assisted us in relocating and provided us with clothing and furniture that included a beautiful vanity dresser for my bedroom. I remember the vanity dresser clearly. We were relocated to an apartment in one of the many housing projects in the inner city. This is where I was raised. In the early sixties, when I was a child, there was racial segregation in this particular housing project, with a black side and a white side. One street separated the buildings, which separated the races. Still I do not recall any racial tension. I guess I can attribute that to the fact that everyone stayed on their respective side. However, I can say in the same breath that we were integrated, as well, because I had just as many white friends as I did black friends since we all went to the same school. By the time I became a teenager, however, there was just a handful of whites still living there.

It goes without saying that my father continued to physically abuse my mother. It seems as though they were fighting every other day. I don't know why, but I don't recall ever questioning my parents about their violent episodes, and I never tried to intervene. Perhaps it was because my mother, in her strange way, would always go out of her way to apologize for my father's disruptive behavior, and she always did so immediately following each one of his explosive, abusive attacks. Without fail, she would sit me down and explain to me that my father had some sort of mental disorder, and that was why he could not control his anger. Consequently, she accepted his abuse and forgave him every time, and for the same reason, she wanted me to forgive him too. I forgave him for her sake and tried to hate him for my sake—if that makes any sense. In that state of confusion and uncertainty, I found that it hurt to love him, and it hurt to hate him.

Following these outrageous, violent acts, my father would begin to wail. He would wail loud enough for the entire world to hear. He did so by begging and pleading for my mother's forgiveness. His piercing, loud guilt-ridden outbursts were the finale of his violent attacks, at least for that moment, until the next time. It astonishes me that my mother rarely displayed anger, simply a tear or two every so often, with her visible bruises. I have vague memories of crying. I suppose I didn't cry for the very reasons that I touched on earlier. For one, when his rampages finally ceased, I could rest assured that my mother would come into my room to comfort me, and amazingly, she would be cleaned up and fully composed by that time. I don't know how she survived the physical violent attacks against her body, mind, and spirit. I marvel when I reflect on my mother and what she has endured in my lifetime. Perhaps her picture will emerge if you search the word *stoic*. I have never seen her break down or lose control. When we were trapped in that burning building, she displayed unwavering calmness and patience. Even during the deaths of her parents and her four sisters, she was a pillar of strength, consoling those of us who were overcome with heartbreak and grief.

During my upbringing, there was no limit to what she would do—in the best way she knew how—to make sure that I felt protected, irrespective of the abusive circumstances my father put us through. To some extent, the way she defended my safety made me perceive our dysfunctional life as normal. She continually put up this huge wall of defense for my father by justifying his actions, while at the same time trying to shield me from the frightening truth about him. In all candor, I found myself utilizing my own defense mechanism because, deep in my heart, I knew his actions were morally wrong.

As the years passed, my mother and I developed a mental telepathy between us concerning his predictable rages. We knew without saying a word; we would simply look at one another and ominously knew what to expect. These anticipated violent attacks usually occurred when he was alcohol or drug induced, after hanging out half the night, bar hopping and partying— especially during the holiday seasons. In the long run, this was a psychological setback for me during my early adult life and, regretfully, during the early years of raising my children. I despised parties and celebrations of any kind because of the horrible memories that plagued me, recalling that joyous celebrations brought on disastrous ends.

When I was a child, as soon as my father walked in the door after his binge drinking, doping, or a combination of both, my mother would tell me to go into my bedroom and close the door, as if my bedroom was soundproof and I couldn't hear what was going on in the next room. At some point I took solace by pushing my fingers as far as they would go into my ears, squeezing my eyelids together as tight as possible, and covering my head with my blankets. I made every effort to drown out the horrific sounds of violence by escaping to the rhythmical sounds that I thought I was imagining. This was my defense mechanism for altering the reality of the violence going on in the next room. As I grew older, I realized that those soothing rhythmical sounds I used as an escape were my heartbeats. It was magical, and nothing short of miraculous, that my heartbeats carried me to a place of peace and serenity.

Meanwhile, in the next room there were violent screams of pain as my mother pleaded for my father to stop hitting her, coupled with the sound of her body being thrashed against every object in her path. By God's grace, I was able to silence the violence when I allowed myself to be carried to a place of tranquility by the sounds of my beating heart. I would remain in this position until I fell asleep or until my father grew tired of hitting her and fell into a drunken stupor. Immediately thereafter, as always, my mother would come into my bedroom to make sure that I was safe and sound, attempting to reassure me that everything was copacetic. After a while, her explanations about his violent behavior became senseless. Sometimes I would feign sleep, and she would quietly close the door. Other times she would come in and lie down beside me, and we would fall asleep together. In spite of everything, she was unyielding in her efforts to convince me to understand him and their volatile relationship.

This may sound strange, but I did not fear my father. I was only afraid of what he would do to my mother. Oftentimes my mother and I would leave the house—escape is a better word for it—before he came home. Then we would return home later that evening or the next day when he sobered up. One night my mother and I literally ran outside into the dark night and waited on a street corner for one of her sisters to rescue us. That night will forever remain imbedded in my mind because, for the first time, I saw fear in my mother's eyes. She was petrified. I don't know what made that night any different from the others. Fear penetrated my bones for the first time, especially since I had never seen my mother show fear until then. She had always displayed such great fortitude, particularly for my benefit. However, that night, my mother cried nonstop and vowed that she would no longer allow him to hurt us. At last, she was weary of the abuse.

I was about eleven years old, and that was the first and only time I have seen my mother overwhelmed with emotion. I will forever be marveled by the woman God has given me for a mother. As for my father, I just wanted him to disappear, and to my amazement, he did—until one day I was confronted with the strange feeling of déjà vu.

DÉJÀ VU

THE PAST IN THE PRESENT, or when it seems that a situation has been lived before, is said to be the definition of déjà vu. I say that to say this:

Suddenly my father wasn't in our lives anymore, and I felt such a great sense of relief. As I remember, I was not concerned about his whereabouts. I was a young child, and I sincerely believed that he was gone because I had wished so many nights that he would not come home, especially pissy drunk. I believed that my wishes had been granted, and he had really disappeared. Then one day, my mother said to me, "We are going to visit your father." Being rattled by that statement, I thought, *What is she talking about?* Why were we going to see him, where, and for what? Being a naive child, I was perplexed. *When someone disappears they are gone forever, right?* At least this is what I wanted to accept as true. Still, confused as ever, I thought, *What is going on?*

I was unaware that during the time he was gone, my father was serving time in jail for domestic violence—finally, the result of my mother filing charges. I say that his absence was unbeknownst to me, but in retrospect I clearly remember my mother explaining to me, in detail, that my father had been put away because he needed help for his bad actions. The fact of the matter was I just chose to block him and his whereabouts out of my mind. I had totally detached myself from him, so it did not matter where he was as long as he was not with us. I had convinced myself that he had just vanished.

The struggle within my heart was I really did not inquire or care about his whereabouts because I did not want to face the fact that there was a remote possibility he still existed and could come back into our lives. I was hoping that he was gone forever, and I was content with that, period. This may sound a little off the wall, especially regarding the physical abuse that he inflicted on my mother, but I never wished that he was dead or that any harm would come his way. I just did not want him around us. I could love him from afar. And I did love him immensely. He was my father. He raised me and protected me to the best of his ability.

My mother instilled that in me my entire life, even though I did not want to hear it. Even without her pounding that message into my head, I knew my father loved us both, and we truly loved him. He was just another human being with unresolved issues from his childhood—issues that set off a mental and violent disorder that, in turn, led to drug and alcohol abuse. Only with time was I able to come to that conclusion. However, I never had the opportunity to express that sentiment of understanding to him before his death. I was still angry and holding on to feelings of resentment, despite the fact that my mother had forgiven him and ultimately divorced him.

On my mother's insistence, I went to visit my father years later in the hospital for the last time. Sadly, he took his last breath that same night. I would like to believe that he recognized me, taking into consideration that he passed away from Alzheimer's disease, a debilitating illness to one's state of mind. Therefore, he was more delusional than anything else. I did have the opportunity to embrace him at that time, with sincere heartfelt love and compassion. It was an unforgettable, unexplainable feeling. It had always hurt to love him, and it had always hurt me to try to hate him. I speak of him more now than I ever have in my life. I can say now that I was honored to be his daughter, a feeling that only developed over time. I know, without a doubt, that he was honored to be my father.

Unbelievably, he and my mother remained close friends until his death. By this time, my amazing mother had become a substance abuse and behavioral counselor. She made his funeral arrangements and delivered the eulogy. Strangely enough, I did not grieve at all during his funeral. I was simply in awe, watching my mother speak with no ill will. However, one morning a few days later, I woke up inconsolable, wishing for him to come back. Life can truly be confusing at times. Years later, as a state police academy graduate and a state corrections officer, I know he would have been full of pride and joy—and deservingly so since he was a major factor in molding me for the rough edges of life. I took heed of his words and actions.

Now I was reporting for duty to one of the most notorious maximum security institutions in the country, a state prison known as the abyss. Upon entering the prison for the first time, slowly but surely I started to feel as though I had been there before—you know, that strange feeling of déjà vu. At the same time, I was overwhelmed by a multitude of emotions. It was my first day on the job inside this massive prison coexisting with, for the most part, committed psychopaths and convicted criminals who were spending the rest of their lives behind bars. I was more confused than ever because, for some reason, besides wanting to be closer to home, I willingly requested and fought for the transfer to this insane asylum of criminal minds. There were other prisons I could have chosen; however, I chose this one.

Once inside, I could sense that this prison was totally unlike the others; it was in a class by itself. It was similar to an enormous zoo, full of strange, loud noises and confusion and disorder. Nonetheless, carrying on the way I did, one would never believe that I had been a corrections officer for almost three years by that time. The conglomerate of my emotions went from bad to worse. When a senior corrections officer locked the final gate leading into the abyss he cunningly blurted out, "You look nervous, Officer. How long have you been with the department?" I was too embarrassed to respond with the truth. Then again, I was well aware that it was an intimidation tactic on his part. As I've explained, the officers were no better than the prisoners in their attempts to intimidate you. Therefore, I responded accordingly, "Don't worry about me; worry about doing your job and secure the gates."

As soon as I heard the loud clicking sound of the gates locking, I was blindsided by a rush of claustrophobia. *Why am I suddenly feeling trapped?* I struggled with myself. Maybe it was because I was locked inside this massive prison that housed twenty-five hundred imposing criminal men—men who were hard-core serial criminals, murderers, rapists, pedophiles, and most of all, violent psychopaths, just to name a few of their traits. These prisoners were the worst of the worst, with nothing better to do than plot, plan, and pump iron all day. After working inside different prisons for the past three years, all of a sudden the inability to leave on my own free will rendered a feeling of captivity and a deep sense of powerlessness. Why? I simply wanted to leave the institution at that very instant, just for a few minutes, so I could feel like I was a civilian and not a prisoner. However, I was a prisoner in all reality until my shift ended.

I guess if I would have screamed loud enough, they would have let me go home but not before relinquishing my badge and picking up my termination papers on the way out. On the contrary, that did not stop me from screaming deep down in my soul. *Help me, somebody. Please, I've made another huge mistake! I really can't do this jail thing anymore!* I was just about to go into a frenzy when I was overpowered by a strong feeling of what I believed to be déjà vu. I swear, I was just about to pee all over myself. I was in a panic mode, looking around for some sort of distraction—looking for a way out in my mind's eye—when I became acutely aware that I had been there before! This was the same prison where my mother brought me to visit my father during his incarceration.

As soon as I received this revelation, I realized I was standing in the exact area where I had stood as a child when I last saw my father in a cognitive state. Right away, the reminiscence of that whole encounter became surreal. I remembered that he had been standing behind steel bars on the very same tier, the roughest tier in the prison, to this day. Even though my father was no longer living, it seemed as if he was alive at that moment, and my last encounter with him was being relived. He was smiling and waving. But most of all, at that moment in time, he was my loving father, and the gentle man that I had known he could be. He was not inebriated or hallucinating from heroin. In the still of that moment, he was full of joy when he called to me from his cellblock. "Utopia, Utopia. Hey, baby girl." Unbelievably, Utopia was his nickname for me. It is unconscionable, but he eloquently discussed this word and its meaning quite often. (Utopia is paradise, heaven, a place or state of perfection.)

What was happening to me was a buildup of memories that I had blocked for so long, and they were now beginning to emerge. For such a long time, I had dismissed the fact that he had even served time in jail, just as I had dismissed everything else about him and his behavior. I was so accustomed to telling the lie that he was never an integral part of my life, and that he had abandoned my mother and me before I was even born. I reiterated this untruth so often that I had persuaded myself to believe it was true, until that day I entered the abyss. As soon as I stepped foot inside of that prison, I was on an emotional roller coaster. I was terrified by my surroundings and puzzled about the recurring effects of déjà vu until I realized it was the last place I had seen my father cognizant. All of this had an emotional impact that immediately reopened the truth about my purposely hidden and forgotten past. Just when it seemed that I was about to burst into tears, my level of fear subsided, and in a startling twist, I was overjoyed to envision my father once again. After all, he was my protector as crazy as that sounds. With the benefit of hindsight, I honestly believed that I was subconsciously seeking his protection at that point, the same way I did when I was a little girl.

I feared nothing when my father and I were out and about. Outside of our tumultuous home, that is. He took me everywhere with him down in the trenches of the ghetto, from the filthy, broken-down bars, where he drank or went into the back and shot up heroin (while a barmaid watched over me), to the pissy alleyways to shoot craps or roll the dice. Wherever we traveled, he had this grip on my hand that was unshakable. He was an imposing figure of a man. I would watch him as he watched or threatened others. "Don't go anywhere near my daughter or I will kill you!" Many times he would take me to the park and hold my hand with that unshakable grip of strength, power, and protection. While strolling along, he would invariably promise me that he would never let anything bad happen to my mother and me, expressing in that same breath how much he loved us both. I know, it sounds insane.

There were times when he would carry me on his shoulders, and I would imagine that I was in that beautiful place of Utopia, the paradise he referred to so often. Meanwhile I would completely void out our unstable home situation. The cruel reminder of our dysfunctional household only came into play when he would binge on alcohol, shoot up heroin, and then take out his frustrations on my mother. As a child listening to my parents' continuous praises and their loving depictions of each other, I guess I chose not to adhere to what I saw. Instead I chose to take the high road, so to speak, and go with what they ingrained in my head, which were fairy tales. This falls in line with one of my mother's most famous phrases: "Do as I say, not as I do." I know it all sounds psychotic, but it's the sad truth.

At any rate, most times during our father-and-daughter moments, and there were many, he was also genuinely contrite with respect to his violent behavior toward my mother. Contrary to what I wrote about him earlier, I failed to mention that he did possess some admirable qualities. Regrettably, I did not come to that appreciation until my revelation in the prison that day. Overall, he was a hardworking man and an overly protective father and husband. It sounds ridiculous, but life's changes sometimes do. Some things you cannot make up or explain. He was a feared man in our poverty-ridden neighborhood, and not too many folks had much to say to my mother or me for that very reason.

What he instilled in me were the worthy qualities that have made me the strong-willed woman I am today. Therefore, when I envisioned him for those few staggering moments, I instantly became tranquil. I felt safe and protected, just as I did when I was a child and we had our happy times together. In spite of his temperament, he taught me self-respect and patience, especially after being compelled to listen to his long lectures about the hardships of life that I would face as a woman. One of his main lessons was "never let a man disrespect you or hit you." I know, again, that it's insane—these words coming from an abuser. I've never been able to wrap my brain around or rationalize the thinking process of my parents and their relationship. I stopped trying to figure that out long ago. Among his many lectures, my father also taught me to always be alert and aware of my surroundings, considering the neighborhood in which we lived and, above all else, the type of company he kept, seeing that he was an alcoholic and a heroin addict. These were his words.

Moreover, he always told me to warn him immediately if someone troubled my mother or me, or if a situation just did not seem right. "Never trust anyone," he imbedded in my brain. "I don't care who it is, including my so-called friends. My friends are not your friends!" He would say this with conviction. "Always walk with your head held high; don't be afraid and show no fear because I will always be there to protect you. Remember—your intuition is your best friend." I would receive that speech almost daily. I trusted everything my father said, including his words of self-sufficiency and self-respect.

These words have supported me throughout my life. Therefore, I attribute much of my perseverance to my father, not only as a female corrections officer, but also as a woman. I know he would have been proud of my life's accomplishments. In saying that, I am at peace with what was a tumultuous family relationship. Only with time, patience, and trust in God have I become grateful to have had him as my father, and just as grateful to have reached this point in my life. I pray he is at peace ... because I am.

RIGHT THEN AND THERE

THERE WAS A MAJOR SNOWSTORM looming on the day I was scheduled for the final phase of testing before being accepted into the State Police Academy. At approximately five o'clock that morning, I received a call from an official with the Department of Corrections (DOC), informing me that the scheduled testing would not be cancelled due to the anticipated inclement weather. Therefore, the sooner I got there, the better. Eager to land the job, I left my home almost immediately. A drive that would normally take about forty-five minutes to an hour took approximately three hours due to the increasing blizzard conditions. It seemed the closer I got to the academy, the worse the conditions became. Right then and there, I should have taken heed because from that day until the day I retired, my career and experience with the DOC was much like that hazardous three-hour drive: risky, dangerous, and nerve-racking.

When I finally arrived at the police academy, I could not get in the door fast enough before an obnoxious female corrections officer greeted me. She handed me a urine analysis container and immediately instructed me to follow her to the bathroom. Oblivious to the procedures, I assumed that she was going to wait outside of the bathroom until I was finished. When I attempted to close the bathroom door, she shoved her foot in the doorway and rudely conveyed that it was standard procedure to leave the bathroom door open so she could observe me giving the urine sample. Supposedly, this procedure prevented foul play. "What? Are you serious?" I shouted in disbelief. She looked at me as if I was stupid for even posing such a question and replied, "You either do it or go home." Mortified with this process, but having no choice in the matter, I relieved myself into the plastic container. I sealed it, cleaned my genital area, and washed my hands. All the while she intently stood in the doorway and scrutinized the process from beginning to end. Totally humiliated, I handed her the container filled with my urine. She abruptly snatched it and walked away like I was an unruly prisoner giving her a hard way to go.

The next phase of this grueling process was a psychological evaluation by the state's psychiatrist, which was, in my opinion, a criminal interrogation. I say this because the questioning seemed more like a criminal suspect's interrogation than a psychological evaluation for employment. This was one of the first inklings, along with the urine analysis fiasco, that made me feel more and more like I was being treated as a prisoner. The psychiatrist's questions were extremely demeaning in nature and downright personal. For the first few minutes, you could not tell me that I was not behind a two-way mirror. I wanted to interject and ask,

"Did I do something wrong? Why am I being interrogated?" However, I knew better.

He and his questions came across in the most condescending manner. He boldly rushed in with "At what age did you start having sex? Are you comfortable in your skin? Are you a racist? What recreational drugs have you used, and how did they make you feel? Have you ever paid for sex, or has anyone ever paid you? How do you feel about homosexuality? Do you keep secrets? In whom do you confide? How many times have you stolen something in your life, and what? Have you ever cheated on an exam, and if so, when and where? What form of discipline did your parents exercise?" These were just some of the questions I can recall off the top of my head. I made every effort to remain as calm as possible. I was highly insulted by his questions and just as insulted by his posture reflecting his arrogance. His whole approach appeared to be unethical. Compelled by sheer humiliation, I mustered up enough nerve to ask this doctor, "Are these questions specifically designed for me, or are they standard for all of the prospective corrections officers?" He made it clear that I better get over myself and proceed with the session, or I could leave and forfeit my opportunity for employment with the DOC. I literally could not afford that, so I complied.

When he was finally finished with his interrogation, I was itching to get out of there and go home. I was under such intense scrutiny for so long that day that I had completely forgotten all about the blizzard conditions outside. What made matters worse, the governor had declared a state of emergency; therefore, I was stranded. Well, the state department was gracious enough to provide an overnight stay at a nearby hotel for everyone taking the test that day.

After going through that entire ordeal, I was somewhat ambivalent about my career as a corrections officer. That night

I pondered whether or not I was suited for the job. I even contemplated rescinding my resignation from my previous employer. I went back and forth the entire night until I came up with the dumbest conclusion. I decided that because I had previously worked as a clerk for the county prosecutor's office and dealt with law enforcement officers and convicted criminals up close and personal, I should be suitable for the job as a corrections officer. Taking all of that into consideration, I believed that I was capable of handling the job, and as a result, I should have no problems. Besides, the salary increase would certainly be financially worthwhile for my children and me. That eye-opener alone superseded all of the above. Still, I did not take into account that my experiences with the criminal justice system and convicted criminals were exclusively on the outside of the prison. Therefore, I lacked the full understanding of being isolated from the outside world behind a ten-foot concrete wall, surrounded by razor wire fencing. In one word: imprisonment.

I did not have a clue as to what I was about to get myself into or what was impending with respect to the life behind the walls of a maximum security prison.

THE TRANSITION

THE TRANSITION FROM WEARING BUSINESS attire—dresses, dress blouses, skirts, and heels—to wearing a bulletproof vest; tactical pants; heavy-duty, high-top, steel-toe boots; police caps; and gloves; coupled with a two-inch-wide tactical equipment belt filled with weaponry, was a significant transition for me. The hardest adjustment was getting accustomed to wearing pants every day. I have always been self-conscious about my backside. I hardly wore pants because they revealed so much of that part of my body. Every now and then, when I chose to wear pants, they would have to be accompanied by a jacket or a long blouse as camouflage. So you can imagine how I felt having to wear a uniform with pants every single day in an environment of predominantly men. There was no way that I could hide my behind this time, something that I'd been doing since I was old enough to choose and wear my own clothing.

Certainly, I was completely aware of the fact that I had to conquer this phobia if I wanted the job. And, as I anticipated, my self-conscious feelings were all over the place when I put on the uniform to report to the police academy. Naturally, the men wasted no time in subjecting me to their lack of respect or innuendoes relating to my protruding butt. However, on the flipside and positive side of things, their antics and comments were to my advantage for it forced me to establish swiftly the most revered principle behind the wall: respect.

THE POLICE ACADEMY

ON MY FIRST DAY IN the police academy, the recruits were instructed to be there at the crack of dawn, in uniform and prepared for inspection. The uniform inspection, along with the instructors' condescending demeanors, spoke volumes about what to expect for the next three months of training and living in the barracks. The instructors strutted around and patronized us about our uniforms, and any other trivial thing they could find insulting, as we stood in humiliation on that brisk October morning. Like newborn animals in the wild, we were considered fresh new meat. Their display of buffoonery was a process of elimination, weeding out recruits by mentally yanking their chains using certain intimidation tactics.

They were condescending toward all of the recruits but more noticeably toward the females. Of the sixty-five recruits, eighteen were females, and more than half of the women were very young. They were either right out of high school or in their early twenties just out of college in search of an interim job. I had just turned thirty years old. I was going through a bitter divorce and had three children. Therefore, I considered myself a little more seasoned when it came to life's experiences, especially because I could sense, almost immediately, that some of the instructors were veterans on the road to retirement. Essentially, it was like a pack of wolves descending upon their prey—namely, the female recruits. My suspicions were right on point, inasmuch as they wasted no time when the lights went out at night. The sexual escapades began to run rampant throughout the barracks. Some of the young ladies were so naive, or just trying to sustain a job, that they would do almost anything to remain in the academy, and the instructors were taking full advantage.

Here we were in an intense training program for the security and safety of a maximum security institution, only to end up being bombarded with having to guard ourselves from the male predators in the academy. What was even more depressing were the limited choices for refuge, seeing that the few female instructors available added insult to injury by flaunting airs of jealousy concerning the new female recruits. I was oblivious then but later learned that the rivalry among the females was indicative of the behavior to expect as a female corrections officer. It is no exaggeration regarding the ongoing dilemmas, convoluted personalities, and awkward issues that the females either put themselves through or had to cope with. If a female felt she could use her body to gain advantage in some way, that notion would inevitably end in disaster. It made no difference if she was naive or weak. In both situations, she would be exploited by the men.

For me, the following episode was the actual premiere of the academy. It was a few weeks into training, and I was genuinely excited about participating in the self-defense course. Well, the course was brought to an abrupt halt when a female instructor alleged that a male self-defense instructor caused her to sprain her ankle. She claimed that he was overly aggressive during a demonstration of a defensive tactical move and wouldn't let up. This incident stirred up a serious discrepancy that led to a series of questioning by higher officials in the DOC. There were about twenty recruits in the class, including myself, who witnessed the training exercise in question. The female instructor had not complained during any of the demonstrations and continued with the exercises for the remainder of class without incident. Then we all returned to our barracks. That being said, no one could attest to her allegations. So, when she came in the next day in an ankle cast and walking on crutches, we wondered what had happened to her overnight. The bottom line to this story is that a secret was slowly unraveling. The secret was that the two instructors were involved in a fateful love affair. He decided that he no longer wanted to sneak around on his wife; therefore, he wanted to break off the relationship. Consequently, she felt jilted and wanted to continue her infidelity, even though she also was married. She sought out revenge by conjuring up this malicious hoax about a sprained ankle, anticipating that he would be suspended or fired. I expected that they both would lose their jobs, but it didn't turn out that way. She was fired for conjuring up a lie and filing a false report. He was transferred to another academy, where he continued to be a self-defense instructor.

Here I was thinking, or better yet hoping, that the urine analysis fiasco and the so-called psychological evaluation I had to endure would be the worst of things, at least until after graduation. I guess I expected too much. The three months I resided in the barracks at the police academy were like being trapped in a college dorm party, plagued with all sorts of improprieties.

Plus, the academy was where would-be corrections officers started dropping out, voluntarily or involuntarily. Some were voluntarily leaving simply because they could not financially afford twelve weeks without a salary, so they left because of the undue stress. Others, admitting defeat, realized that this was not the job for them. There were other recruits who left involuntarily by way of dismissal for violations, including but not limited to cheating or failing a test; engaging in sexual misconduct, drunkenness, physical and verbal altercations; and, showing contempt. The list goes on. Despite these infractions, there were two major violations that stood out the most: failing to qualify on the shooting range and illegal drug use. Both infractions resulted in an immediate dismissal.

For sure, I was one of those on the threshold of dismissal for failing to qualify on the shooting range—or simply bailing out, due to my unforeseen anxiety associated with handling a gun. Firearms practice outdoors on the range was mandatory training for the last two weeks in the academy, regardless of inclement weather conditions. My class started in the beginning of October and ended in December. Therefore, I was on the range for the last two weeks in the wintry month of December. We were training to qualify and carry 9 mm semiautomatic pistols, M16 rifles, and shotguns. On that account, I will be forever grateful to an honorable lieutenant who tirelessly worked with me until I was competent and confident enough to pass on the range. For those last fourteen days, he went out of his way to make sure I was practicing before and after the standard target-shooting exercises. In frigid temperatures, rain and snow, it did not matter.

I was carrying on like a young adolescent, ranting and raving and looking for an excuse to quit. "Just because something is hard doesn't mean that you have to quit," he said repeatedly. It was just the two of us, and his patience definitely exceeded my weakness. After throwing tantrums like a spoiled brat, he would say, still in his monotone voice, "When you're done, I want you to concentrate, aim, and shoot." He treated me as if I was his own daughter, and I respected him accordingly.

From the very start, I was having trouble aiming steadily at the target. Another range instructor assisted me at first, but he was more focused on my backside than on my shooting abilities. While I was aiming for the target, he was aiming for sex. His sly innuendoes did not help my concentration at all. The lieutenant noticed how uncomfortable I was and asked what was going on. To be honest, I didn't tell him how the instructor was constantly in my ear, complimenting me on my backside and asking, "When you gonna let me hit that?" Telling him, "Never," was like talking to a brick wall. I thought I could get through the outdoor practices, but, like I said, handling the weapon was throwing me off as well. I explained to the lieutenant that I was just uncomfortable with this particular instructor. The lieutenant pretty much caught my drift and took over. I'm sure that's why he was concentrating on us anyway. I'm just grateful that he took charge.

During firearms practice, we were trained to shoot the weapons from different positions—obviously from a standing position, as well as on our knees and lying facedown on the ground. The weather conditions had no impact on the two-week schedule on the outdoor range. Meanwhile, my body was shivering from the bone-chilling concrete. The worst of these positions, for me, was on my knees. The pain was agonizing. I was crying so much that I could barely see the targets, because my eyes were flooded with tears. We were not permitted to wear gloves, and because of that, my fingers were not only swollen but also riddled with multiple cuts and bruises from constantly squeezing the trigger to shoot off hundreds of rounds. This occurred from sunrise until sunset. At that point, we were required to wear night vision goggles in order to see the targets in the dark. Keep in mind, I was going out on the range twice as much in that two-week period with the lieutenant, given that I was on the brink of being kicked out.

By the end of the first week, the guns began to feel heavier and heavier, making it a struggle to lift and hold them with a steady and firm grip. I was squeezing the trigger so many times that my forefinger became stiff and numb. It was becoming more and more difficult to bend. It felt like it was frostbitten and about to be severed. Last, but not least, having to dive facedown or on my knees onto the cold, wet dirt in the mud, snow, sleet and rain—wearing what felt like a ton of weaponry gear—was nothing short of torture.

After the first couple of days, I felt excruciating pain in my knees, elbows, and hands. There was nothing I could do to alleviate the pain in my hands because they were exposed. However, I was able to ease the pain in my knees and elbows. I took the chance and by secretly wearing unauthorized knee and elbow pads underneath my uniform. Thank God, the instructors never checked. In addition, I wore an unauthorized makeshift pad that was really a sanitary pad with adhesive strips. I wedged the sanitary pad in the pectoral area of my chest between my bra and the bulletproof vest to minimize the forceful recoil of the rifle and shotgun. Eventually I got through the two weeks with the lieutenant's intensive help, and I passed. However, it was protocol for all corrections officers to qualify every six months, and I dreaded it. I never really overcame the psychological aspects of handling a gun. I will get into that much later in my narrative.

The second major infraction, the most shameful and indefensible one, was for illegal drug use. During the twelve-week training period, we were given several random drug tests. Unbeknownst to the recruits, the test results were not disclosed until a week or so before graduation. This implied to the drug users that their test results came back negative, so they carried on, participating in the graduation practices. If that was not humiliating enough, the DOC further coaxed additional drug users by withholding their failed test results right up to the morning of graduation. And this is why I consider it the most shameful infraction, besides being indefensible. The instant a recruit was informed that he or she had failed the drug test, the recruit was automatically escorted off of the state grounds by two superior officers. If, in fact, the situation went from controlled to chaos, the local police were called to assist in an arrest. As a consequence, the recruit was handcuffed and jailed.

Due to the element of surprise and the manner in which things were handled, I don't have to tell you that on nearly every occasion, the situation did go from controlled to chaotic. Form a mental image of this if you can. After three months of intense training and living in the barracks away from your family and friends, you are totally prepared to finally graduate. Euphoria is setting in, and your family and friends are eagerly waiting in the graduation hall. Out of nowhere, you are summoned to report to the superintendent's office, where you are informed that you will not be participating in the graduation ceremony, already in progress. Furthermore, you are terminated because you failed the drug test. To add to this devastating news, there is a great possibility that you may be jailed for the felony offense of possession of a controlled dangerous substance on state property. You are then escorted back to the barracks to retrieve your personal belongings. Subsequently, you are handcuffed and escorted off the grounds. Mind you, this happens in the presence of other recruits and anyone else who may be in the vicinity. Then the superintendent personally notifies your family that you will not be participating in the graduation and requests that they politely leave the premises.

One dares not ask questions during this whole process. You mind your own business (MYOB), another code of behavior. It did not matter if you knew or not, one would soon find out that there are no secrets in the academy or in the prisons, being that they are synonymous with one another. It was emotionally distressing on all accounts from beginning to end. To see someone whom you have befriended and bunked with for three months being led away like a prisoner in an officer's uniform is an undignified way to go out. Unfortunately, it came to be common practice when I went behind the wall.

Disheartening is the only word that comes to mind when I think back on how the training in the police academy began and how it ended on the day of graduation. It was supposed to be the beginning of a rewarding career, but it appeared as if the DOC made every effort to dehumanize the recruits in order to compel them to either perform better or get out. For obvious reasons, it was not going to get any better.

ORIENTATION

GRADUATING FROM THE POLICE ACADEMY was a bittersweet experience. I was especially relieved that I did not have to go back out on the shooting range, at least not for the next six months. However, before reporting to our assigned institutions, we were obligated to attend a two-week orientation inside a maximum security prison. It was my first experience with incarcerated prisoners, other than my father. Three other recruits and I decided to carpool. I could not believe it; I was officially a rookie corrections officer. I was eager to work since there was so much talk about plenty of overtime, and money was my main reason for taking the job in the first place.

After leaving the human resources department where we received our badge numbers, we were directed to the photo room to obtain our picture identification cards. I started feeling more and more energetic. I was so proud of myself. It was such an accomplishment after an incredibly challenging experience in the academy. I was beginning to feel somewhat comfortable. I was also sensing negative vibes when passing through the mass movement of prisoners, and those vibes were not coming from the prisoners.

I was the first rookie instructed to go into the photo room to have my ID picture taken. A sergeant and a prisoner sat at a table behind a camera. I was surprised to see a prisoner in the room. It was apparent that the sergeant noticed the perplexed look on my face when he stated, "You can have a seat; just look into the camera." I was shocked when the prisoner snapped my picture, and it was evident in my photo. I honestly thought it was a prank. That would not have been unusual because practical jokes were common as an initiation for incoming rookies, but this was not one of them. The sergeant would not allow me to retake my picture. After grasping that this was legit, the prisoner had the nerve to ask me, "What's your full name and badge number?" Despicably, I replied, "Excuse me?" As he gestured to respond, the sergeant intervened and sternly said, "He needs your information so he can complete the process of laminating your ID card. So again, state your name and badge number to the prisoner." *This can't be standard procedure*, I thought as I complied and questioned myself at the same time. *I am being ordered by a sergeant to divulge my personal information to a prisoner. Shouldn't I be asking the prisoner for his ID and his inmate number?* This was merely another example of the many similarities between a prisoner and a corrections officer, which I found to be a regular course of practice.

Naturally, the other rookies were just as shocked to have a prisoner take their ID picture. This became one of the hot topics for discussion on our drive home, among the other chain of shocking events that occurred throughout our two weeks of orientation. While touring the jail, walking from tier to tier, all eyes were on us. We were being gazed upon as if we were aliens from another planet. To my surprise, most of the piercing stares were coming from the officers. I could understand if those stares came from the prisoners; however, I could not make sense of the piercing stares, along with the negative vibes, coming from the officers. As a new rookie, I expected to receive warm welcomes from our peers. On the contrary, I could count on one hand how many handshakes or cordial greetings I received from my new coworkers. In fact, during our tour we were taken to a reception room, where we could not sit down fast enough before a self-absorbed lieutenant began addressing the class. He literally pointed out certain rookies, whom he deemed would not succeed as a corrections officer, just by looking at them. His whole approach was ludicrous. When he pointed at me, he yelled, "And you! You are too pretty!"

I was not only insulted by his remark but at a loss for words. I was totally embarrassed. I did not have a good comeback, so I just sat there looking stupid with the rest of his victims. He continued to rant while feeding his ego. Then he came up to me, leaned over, and said, "You should be flattered!" His disposition caught me completely off guard, and I was about to strike back in retaliation when I remembered what my mother always said, "Taste your words before you spit them out." Taking that heed of caution, I adjusted my thoughts and said with composure, "With all due respect, sir, I am going to do my best to succeed." He smirked and said, "Yeah right, we'll see."

To my dismay, it began to sink in more and more that this was the type of unwarranted behavior I would have to endure as a female corrections officer. I was still ignorant to the magnitude it would scale, specifically coming from the officers. I was prepared for the prisoners. I was in no way prepared for the tidal wave that would come from my colleagues. And the shock waves kept coming.

On that first day, the three rookies and I decided that we were going to go out for lunch. We anticipated that going out to eat would help us to relax and unwind. That anticipation was cut short when we were informed precisely at lunchtime that we were not allowed to leave the prison until our shift ended. According to prison policies, we had to eat lunch inside the prison. At first, this was not a huge disappointment. I thought, *I'll just purchase something in the cafeteria for the time being, assuming there is a cafeteria for the employees.* Except I forgot that I did not have any cash because cash was not allowed inside the prison since it was regarded as contraband.

I was thrown for a loop when I learned that there was not a cafeteria but instead an officers' mess hall. The term *mess hall* did not sit right with me at all; it was a complete turnoff. I was under the impression that mess halls were exclusively for prisoners. What made matters worse, while en route to the officers' mess hall, we were told that the food they were trying to force us to eat was *prepared* and *served* by the *prisoners*. Instantly I lost my appetite. Just the mere thought of having a prisoner prepare my food and serve me was mind-boggling. For an officer to be in accord with this procedure, as if they were dining in a five-star restaurant, was beyond my comprehension. Most prisoners despised corrections officers. Was it me? Having no choice in the matter, we frustratingly made our way to the officers' mess hall.

When we walked inside, I was mesmerized by the unashamed segregation among the officers—black officers on one side and white officers on the other side. If I didn't know any better, I would have thought they were required to sit in these groups of ethnicities. Usually in the workplace, supervisors congregated, but they too were sitting with their own ethnic group. Now I was really feeling out of place, standing with the three rookies with whom I was carpooling, because among the four of us, two were white and two were black. Seeing that we were rookies, we stuck out like sore thumbs, so the four of us just huddled together at a small (dirty) table until lunch was over. None of us ate a thing. The intricacy of what goes on behind the wall is endless. I wondered what would happen during a riot when the prison was on lockdown. Would the officers allow racial tension to divide them in such a life-threatening situation? Hopefully, during those critical times, it would be officers versus prisoners, not blacks versus whites. I cannot highlight enough the complexities of working in such a volatile world and facing the diverse challenges therein. Too often, my experiences with the DOC prompted me to think of the metaphor "trust on life support." For the record, during my tenure as a corrections officer, I never ate the food prepared by the prisoners. From that day forth, I adjusted my eating habits to coincide with my work schedules.

When I first began working my assigned duties, the officers had the option of bringing something small inside to eat, such as a sandwich and a plastic bottle of water or juice. Therefore, I brought something for lunch and something to hold me over until my shift ended. It was not too long after I started my employment with the department that those privileges came to a screeching halt after officers were caught smuggling in contraband. The harsh reality is that the officers are one of the main sources used to smuggle in the deadly contraband that seeps throughout the prisons. Officers of all ranks would give each other courtesy searches or flimsy pat frisks to allow in extra food, as well as deadly weapons, drugs, and money. This is just a fraction of what was illegally trafficked. Consequently, the officers had to conform to a more thorough and detailed pat frisk, in conjunction with a body scan, before entering the institution. This is right in line with what I will continue to point out, and that is the similarities between the officer and the prisoner.

Like other officers, I found ways to smuggle in food small enough to fit in, of all places, the pouch of my bulletproof vest. When I found myself hungry or if commanded to work overtime, having that small stash of food made a big difference. I was determined not to eat or drink anything provided by the state and designed for the prisoners. This was a period in time when I definitely maintained my weight.

But on a serious note, words cannot describe the feelings I had being on the sidelines and watching other officers being handled like prisoners and criminals. By the same token, it was disgraceful to see officers behaving like prisoners and criminals. Contraband infiltrated the prison and could be transported by anyone who entered from the outside world. There were no exceptions, be it officers, civilian employees, visitors, attorneys, doctors, administrative and medical staff, maintenance workers, volunteers, and even clergy and children. If every person who entered was properly and thoroughly searched, there would be far less crime and violations behind the wall. Too often corrections officers were strip-searched, handcuffed, and jailed for smuggling in the most lethal contraband. It's frightening, but it's true.

The fact of the matter is illegal trafficking is extremely detrimental to everyone behind the wall. It subjects those who enter the institutions to the same dangers we face on the streets. One of my interpretations of prison life is "street life confined." The only difference is you stand more of a chance to survive on the streets as opposed to being trapped inside, where you cannot get out and have nowhere to run.

In closing this chapter, I also have to point out that this is a catch-22 situation. Not all lethal items brought into the prison are illegal. There are lethal items that are legally permissible and can be purchased by the prisoner through the inmate commissary. The inmate commissary is a prison store funded for the prisoners by the state, family, friends, and the prisoners themselves. Some items that are sold there can be considered contraband and used as deadly weapons—namely, razor blades, can openers, cans, and other materials that are used to create weapons known as shanks. The list of things and the prisoner's ingenuity behind them are limitless.

RESPECT

MY PARENTS, CONTRARY TO THEIR actions, described the word *respect* to me. Therefore, for me to comprehend the full meaning of respect was another catch-22 situation. I listened to my parents say one thing and then watched them do another in their physically abusive relationship. It was disturbing to watch my father physically abuse my mother and equally disturbing to watch my mother allow the abuse. Ironically, they both ended their lectures on life with the same theme "Do as I say, not as I do." Inevitably, after many years of perplexity and having to learn the hard way by getting involved in an abusive relationship. Only then was I able to decipher their statement and come to its full understanding. It was baffling, to say the least, but imagine having to live with it.

With that being said, the concept of respect and my parents' interpretation of it reverberated through my soul more than ever during my abusive relationship and acrimonious divorce. And I was taking on the position of a corrections officer simultaneously. Understanding the concept of respect, as a woman in a relationship with a man, is of the utmost importance. This is something that has to be established at the onset of the relationship. The same must be incorporated in her position as an officer at the gates of the prison. Still, the reality is that regardless of this upright moral principle, prison is an environment that is prone to death and violence, and I never lost sight of that. Upholding that respect is another story, which brings me to my case in point.

In the previous chapter, I spoke of the three rookies and I, carpooling for our two weeks of orientation. As luck would have it, when the orientation was completed, we were all assigned to the same prison for our ninety-day probation. Hence, we continued to carpool. As time went on, the four of us became closer friends. One day, one of the men expressed he wanted more than just a platonic friendship and invited me out on a date. I wasted no time in declining his invitation. Furthermore, before going into the police academy, I'd made a conscious decision not to become involved with anyone on the job. I was already going through a nasty divorce, and dating was the last thing on my mind. The young man who asked me out was persistent and would not accept no for an answer. After my repeated refusals, his persistence became pushy and inappropriate. Therefore, I made the decision not to carpool with them anymore, and began driving alone.

In spite of that adjustment, he continued to harass me because we would occasionally run into one another when reporting for lineup. In his pathetic attempts, he tried to convince himself and me that my rejections would eventually give in to his swagger. In his perverted way of thinking, he explained, "You know that when a woman says no, she really means yes." He was starting to infringe on my personal space, and I seriously wanted to report him for sexual harassment. It seemed that no matter what I did or said, he was unfazed and persisted. I concluded that he was just that shallow or teetering on the borderline of psychosis. In spite of this, I was apprehensive about rushing to report him since we were both rookies on a ninety-day probation. Additionally, due to the fact that we were in a predominantly male atmosphere, the department was constantly receiving sexual harassment reports from the female corrections officers and employees.

The prison was inundated with the cat-and-mouse game. Consequently, I was inclined to believe that my situation was susceptible to "his word against mine," or a "he said, she said" drama dispute, subjecting us both to termination. Even though I did not care if he was fired or not, at that point I just wanted him to stop stalking me. I was in between a rock and a hard place. I made many attempts to tactfully handle the situation to no avail. In the long run, I was compelled to express how much I was annoyed with the whole ordeal and threatened him to stay away from me, or I would have no other choice but to file a report for sexual harassment. I anticipated that putting him on notice would deter him, and he would back off and leave me alone.

We avoided each other for a short period, but that was virtually impossible. This became uncomfortably evident when he and I were scheduled to work on the same tier as partners for a day. Usually there were senior officers in the area to monitor the rookies, who were still in training. On this day, however, it was decided that we should be able to execute our duties without supervision. I was assigned to walk the tier, and he was assigned to work inside of the control booth, which was locked and secured. His job function was, at my direction, to work the control panel, which controlled the cell doors of one hundred prisoners. My job function was to walk up and down the tier and assist the prisoners as they entered and exited their cells to use the showers and the phones and to complete their job duties. All this was done while they roamed freely on the tier, putting me in a highly vulnerable position.

To achieve these functions, my duty was to call on the radio or signal the officer in the control booth (which was him), indicating which cell gate to open or close by using the controls. This job assignment entailed some serious teamwork. The setup was extremely dangerous for an experienced officer, let alone an inexperienced rookie like myself. The protocol should have called for no less than two officers on the tier. However, it looked to be regular practice to place a novice female rookie in the most volatile positions. Meanwhile, the male rookie was placed in the control booths, where he was safe and secure, no matter what happened.

There was no sense of complaining. I opted to become a corrections officer, knowing full well the potential dangers. Additionally, wherever an officer was assigned to work, they had better get there without hesitation and no questions asked or be prepared to receive their walking papers. Especially a female officer, whose head stayed on the chopping block, so to speak, constantly trying to prove herself. In the meantime, the men would be patiently anticipating her breakdown or failure, so he could come to her rescue and use his so-called protection or assistance as a bartering tool for sexual favors—or take that chance to taunt her. "I told you, women don't belong here."

Meanwhile, hours had gone by, and I was pacing up and down the tier amid the prisoners all by my lonesome. I could not help thinking about the possibility of being assaulted and trapped in a hostage situation. However, we were well into the shift, and on the surface of things, it looked as if my partner/stalker had pushed his personal feelings to the side. Our work assignment was going well until it was time for me to go on break. Before I could leave the tier, it was protocol to make sure that each prisoner was locked in his cell, with the assistance of the officer at the control panel, who electronically locked each cell door. In addition, I had to ascertain that each cell door was secured by manually double-locking it and yanking each gate, subsequent to walking the length of the tier from back to front and making my way towards the control booth, where I would exit. Once I reached the booth he was supposed to automatically unlock the gate enabling me to exit the tier, except, I had to ask him to unlock the gate. To my utter surprise, he refused, and added, "When you turn that "no" into a "yes", and go out to dinner with me, I will let you out."

Unwilling to accept his sheer lunacy, I stood there in awe. In view of that, he felt it necessary to repeat his idiotic request, and this time in a more aggressive tone as if I did not hear him the first time. Clearly, there is never room for horseplay inside a maximum security prison. So I tried my best to downplay the situation in a calm and tactful manner. Nevertheless, the more I asked him to stop horsing around, unlock the gate, and let me out, the more defiant he became, escalating the situation. This went on for a few minutes, and then, unexpectedly a prisoner who overheard our heated discussion yelled from his cell, "Hey, man, let her out and stop playing games!" That's when I gestured to call over the radio for assistance, and he promptly unlocked the gate with a sly grin on his face. Enraged, I marched straight to the main office to file a sexual harassment report. That was it!

The consequences did not matter to me at that juncture. Not only was he in over his head, but he also was putting my safety in imminent danger by horsing around while I was locked on the tier. To add to this heightened situation, even a prisoner felt compelled to intervene on my behalf, opposing his antics. The only drawback was that it could have come back to bite me if I allowed it to. What I mean is if the prisoner was looking for a favor in return, he could have tried to use his involvement as a bargaining tool. In this case, the prisoner was being sincere when he attempted to defuse the situation. This would prove to be one of the many times that a male prisoner chose to stand up for me and other female officers against one of our corrupt male counterparts. What's more, if it were not for the fact that the prisoners overheard the entire ridiculous dispute between the officer and I, I believe that the outcome would have been much different, and not in my favor.

I didn't know whom I could trust. Was this a game where both men were trying to undermine me? The trust factor alone was extremely stressful behind the wall. In an ironic twist, I was writing my first disciplinary report on a corrections officer. I could not understand what was on this man's mind, other than the fact that he was struggling with a bruised ego. While in the process of writing the report, the captain approached me and asked if he could speak with me in private—specifically, after I finished writing my report but before handing it in. Oblivious to his line of attack, and I emphasize the word *attack*, I was ready for just about anything at that point. However, before I allowed my personal feelings to get in the way of my professionalism, I asked him to give me a few extra minutes to gather my thoughts. Actually, I was taking into account that I was going to be criticized by his male chauvinistic opinion with my termination to follow.

To my surprise, he and I sat down and civilly discussed the situation from beginning to end. At that time, I had no idea that he had already been on the tier and had spoken with several prisoners, including the male officer involved. I was not the least bit surprised when he explained to me that the officer told him that I was the one stalking him, and that he'd had enough of trying to persuade me to back off. Little did the officer know, and fortunate for me, the captain had already spoken with several prisoners on the tier before speaking to him, and they conveyed to the captain exactly what happened. Thankfully, their accounts of that little clash corroborated mine.

The captain also informed me that the prisoners were under the impression that I was the officer's wife. He further explained in questioning the prisoners, he found out that the officer was the one spreading this outrageous lie and was doing so in a threatening manner. He was warning the prisoners to stay away from me because he was my husband. That concocted story left me tongue-tied. I had no idea that all of this was going on.

After the captain finished bombarding me with that startling piece of information, he said in the same breath, "So now, what are you going to do to solve this issue?" I was already dazed by everything that he was saying, and then he stumped me with that question. He went on to say, "With all that I've heard and seen thus far, I am making you the officer in charge of this situation. You have conducted yourself in a very professional manner, and I am impressed with what I see in you as an officer. Therefore, I believe that I can trust your decision. So, what is it going to be?" Before I could process what was happening, he had more to say. "There are definitely grounds for his immediate termination on the mere fact that he is still on probation. More than likely, there will be pending criminal charges due to the nature of the offense you have imposed. Or else I can speak to him, and I assure you that he will never harass you again. I guarantee you that he will give you the respect you so deserve. I am certain of it! Your decision will be the deciding factor though, no questions asked. Now, what will it be? I want you to step out of the situation and put yourself in my shoes. Imagine that you are the officer in charge right now," he explained.

I was totally worn down by the whole gamut of things. I felt like collapsing and crying out like a child, "Can I go home now?

I don't want to play this game anymore!" I didn't know what to think. Was this some sort of setup? I felt so defenseless. After being lost in thought for what seemed like an eternity and feeling pressured, apprehensively I went out on a limb and gave him an answer. "I'll be straightforward. It is not my intention to have the officer lose his job. I simply demand to be respected. It's obvious that he's not use to rejection or respecting women. You've assured me that you can bring him down to earth, and I believe in second chances. For that reason, I trust that you will do what you say you can do. I would hate to see him lose his job because of a bruised ego. I think he just has some growing up to do."

Frankly, I felt that he would be the cause of his own demise anyway. Without hesitation, the captain shook my hand and said, "I respect your decision, and I expected no less coming from you. You are going to do well in your career as a corrections officer." Right away he summoned for the officer to come to his office, all before I could express my gratitude for his words of encouragement. Then I started to wonder. What have I opened myself up to? For a while, I was feeling that I had left myself wide open for something else. What? I did not know. Soon thereafter, I was impressed that the officer actually humbled himself and was sincerely contrite. He told me that the captain explained to him what I proposed. He also said to me, "I give you the utmost respect for giving me a second chance. I don't know what came over me." He didn't go into detail about the specifics of their conversation, but from that day forth, he was a reformed man. The incident was never mentioned again, and we continued to work together as if nothing happened. At the end of our probationary period, we were transferred to different institutions, at which time, we wished each other well.

It was not long after having that intense, praiseworthy discussion with the captain that I was assigned to work on a different tier. This time I was called off my post to report to the warden's office. My first thoughts were, *The warden's office? Here we go again. I thought this mess was over and done with! I knew I left myself wide open after that discussion with the captain.* I continued looking for fault until I found myself knocking on the warden's office door.

As I entered his dreary office, I could see that the warden, the captain, and about six other high-ranking officers were present. They all gave the impression that they were patiently anticipating my arrival. Gradually, I began to recognize that I was there for something altogether different from what I assumed. A feeling of despair instantly shot through my veins when I saw the captain who had given me so much encouragement just a few weeks earlier handing me the phone. "You have a phone call," he said in a calm, measured tone. Nervously, I asked, "Who is it? Who could it possibly be?" My entire body turned stiff and my feet would not allow me to take another step. I assumed the worst. Something must have happened to my children. Notably, when I looked around the room, every single one of the officers had the same dismal expression on their faces. Then I panicked and frantically exclaimed, "Did something happen to my children? Are my children all right? What's going on?" The captain, whom I thought I could trust, gave me the vaguest response while shaking his head and shrugging his shoulders. "I don't know what's going on," he replied. Then he stepped closer, pushing the phone closer to my face.

In that short span of time, I had persuaded myself that something had horribly gone wrong and it involved one or all of my children. What else could have been urgent enough to pull me from my post for a phone call in the warden's office? I was only a few steps away from the captain, yet it seemed as though he was a mile away. My boots felt like they were filled with wet cement as I struggled to take a step to retrieve the phone. Hesitantly, I grabbed the phone, and scared to death, I muttered, "Hello?" A man on the other end responded, addressing me by my name. I asked, "Who is this?" "This is the deputy warden," he offhandedly replied. I cried out, "What is going on? Are my children all right?" He sounded surprised when he responded, "Oh no! This has nothing to do with your children." I sighed with relief but was overcome with curiosity.

Before I could find out the purpose for his call, he asked me, "What are your off days?" Still baffled, I answered, "Tuesdays and Wednesdays, sir." He responded, "Oh great! So you are off tomorrow?" I slowly responded, "Yeees?" I was stupefied; he had to know the answers to these simple, clear-cut questions that were so imperative, I had to be pulled from my post. Apparently, the senior officers who filled the warden's office were just as dumbfounded, including the captain and the warden. Or were they? The answer to that I will never know.

Anyway, the vague conversation and the unclear questioning between the deputy warden and I continued. "Do you know where the Holiday Inn Hotel is located by the airport?" he asked. Now excited, I responded, "Yes, of course I do!" I had the asinine thought that I must have been selected to participate in some sort of rookie seminar since that was where the DOC usually held their seminars. Long story short, that thought was quickly shattered because his next statement blew me away when he blatantly stated, "I like the way you look. I think you are a beautiful woman, and I want to spend some time with you, alone, in my hotel room."

While he babbled on, numbness was settling into my bones. At the same time, I was scanning the room like a contestant on a game show, looking out into the audience for help with an answer to a question. The audience in this case was the officers in the room waiting to hear my response, I believed. In the interim, the curiosity was killing me. Did they know the deputy warden's intentions? Did they know what he was saying on the other end of the phone? I wasn't going to ask them—that was for sure. I immediately came back down to earth when he stressed, "Did you get the room number?" I responded with the first thing that popped into my head. "Yes sir! I can hear you." On the surface of things, I was in a tight spot with an observant audience. Let it be understood that I mumbled quite a few expletives under my breath, telling him where he could go stick it, while strategically thinking about my next move or statement.

His overconfidence progressed as he stated, "So pack a bag, and I will meet you there tomorrow night at ten. You don't have to worry about checking in; just come to the room. I'll be waiting for you." When he stopped talking, I felt defeated. I felt as though I had been knocked out even before the bout began. Moreover, not knowing how to handle the overall set of circumstances at that moment, I didn't know what else to say, especially in front of an audience, his posse. Therefore, I figured I'd throw everyone off course and simply countered with a smile. Then I said, "Okay, thank you so much. I appreciate your call," and I hung up the phone.

All at once "you could hear a mouse pissin' on cotton," as my grandmother would say. There was no question that they were eagerly waiting for me to disclose the subject matter of our conversation. However, before I could make my great escape, the captain was bold enough to make it his business to probe. "What was that all about?" he said. Without skipping a beat, I answered, "He commended me on my shooting score at the range." I have no idea how and why that thought came into play. I had one of the worst, if not the worst, scores on the range. In all seriousness, I had to leave that room and their prying eyes immediately to avoid any other questions. Using the excuse that I was in a hurry to use the restroom, I dashed out the door. It was next to impossible for me to remain in that office for another second, unless they physically held me down. I was one step away from a mental meltdown.

Once I reached the bathroom, it took every nerve and fiber in my life's form not to explode into tremendous anger. I had no other choice but to compose myself. I had to go back on post, but my brain was in overload. By no means was I going to meet this sleazeball in a hotel! Where did he get the gall? I was certain that I would be standing in the unemployment line in the very near future. How in the world was I going to rationalize a conversation between the deputy warden of the Department of Corrections and myself? He was the commissioner's right-hand man. I was a female rookie. It was as if I had been seriously wounded and left stranded to die with no help in sight. It was a good thing that it wouldn't be much longer before my shift ended because it was hard for me to function from that point on.

As soon as my shift ended, I logged out, turned in the keys, and rushed to my car, hoping no one wanted to stop and fraternize. I jumped into my car and sped off. Considering that the tears were streaming down my face like pouring rain, I had to pull off to the side of the road and pull myself together. All I could think about was my children and finding another job, paying my mortgage, getting through my divorce ... my entire future. The next two days were my allotted days off, which gave me a chance to regroup. On those two days, I racked my brain, speculating on what to do next. I roamed my house aimlessly. I prayed that he would not be bold enough to call my home once he realized that I was not going to show up at the hotel. If he called, I would have been on my turf, and I was sure that I would have read him the riot act. Overall, I was at a loss, not knowing what to do or in whom to confide.

I wanted and needed my job. Nonetheless, I was not going to sexually appease a man in order to keep it. The sexism was unreal, and this was just the beginning. I intended on speaking to the captain, except he was the one who informed me of the phone call, and that made me feel quite uneasy. I knew if I mentioned the conversation to my coworkers, whom I did not know well enough to divulge such a divisive matter, they would think it was a joke or spread ugly rumors. (I have never discussed this incident to anyone until now.) I started second-guessing myself. *What am I doing to give these men the impression that I am sexually promiscuous?* However, I shunned that thought instantly. I knew it was not something I was doing.

The truth of the matter was that I was surrounded by a bunch of chauvinistic men. Sexual objectification is a better term. Too many of them, look at us as simply an instrument of sexual pleasure, a mere object to be used, as if we have no feelings, or better yet, as if we should not display our feelings at all. Too many believe that women are supposed to be subservient, submissive, and sexually promiscuous—to be ready and willing at their slightest gesture or invitation.

With all due respect to the noble men of the world, I had to accept the fact that I was dealing with a large number of men, and there was no distinction between them. This is something you'll see me going over and over again because it's something that the women of the world, young and old, have to be made aware of. The dishonor was that the only problem I was having so far was with the officers. I was astounded and never expected to be in constant battle with my peers. It had never crossed my mind. It became a weight that was nearly unbearable. I was merely a rookie trying to get through my ninety days of probation. I just wanted to work, get paid, and take care of my children.

You'll see me mentioning the similarities between the officers and the prisoners quite often. But the more I wrote about my experiences as a female corrections officer, the more conscious I became of what I had to go through with my colleagues, as opposed to the prisoners. These were people I had to entrust with my life, without thinking about it. Actually, I was contemplating giving up, throwing in the towel, purely because of the officers' sexual improprieties, not to mention the corruption. I was certain that the incident with the deputy warden was the straw to break the camel's back. I was convinced that I had no recourse and that he would find a way to fire me. Obviously, it would not have been difficult in his position. Anyway I was not about to stoop to his indecent proposal and thus stood my ground. I was relieved that he did not call my home. But then again I still didn't know his next move. It was like playing a game of chess, and it was his turn to make a move—and he did.

My two days off were over, and it was time for me to return to work after engaging in that obnoxious conversation with him. I had only seen him once, and that was when I graduated from the academy. I was told that he rarely visited the prisons. On this day, he deemed it necessary to show his repulsive face. I wondered, *Why?* I assumed that he had come up with something to terminate me. When I reached the prison, there was a big buzz going around about his impending visit. "Spread the word: I heard the DW is coming to the jail today, so be on your best behavior." Everyone was running around like chickens with their heads cut off, trying to make things appear perfect. All I was thinking about was finding another job. However, observing everyone in such a ruckus, I started feeling invigorated. Now I was kind of glad that I had the willpower to return to work and face whatever consequences he had in store for me.

Noticing how everyone was sucking up and willing to do anything to gain his approval made me sick to my stomach.

Therefore, I made up my mind that I was not going to let this bully continue to intimidate me as he was doing to everyone else. I was ready to make a stance and fight for my job. I found it despicable that the entire institution was in such an uproar over this man's cameo appearance. I have never been a brownnoser, and I was not about to start that day or any other time in my life. The more I watched in disgust, the more I started to feel a sense of courage instead of fear. I began to feel emotionally resilient and stronger within. It seemed as though everyone was carrying on like slaves for a slave master. The thought was revolting, knowing the way he had approached me with his sexual ploy. His reason for his surprise visit was to assess the new rookies. Really?

It finally came time to line up for roll call. I was ready. For what, I didn't know, but I was ready. When he came into the room, he began walking down the formation line of rookies, greeting them one by one. The closer he came toward me, the more my knees began to buckle. My whole future was at stake. When he finally approached me, he looked straight into my eyes, and like two boxers before a boxing match, we stared each other down. Then he blurted out, loud enough for the world to hear, "Good afternoon to you, Miss Rookie!" Stern as I could possibly be, I answered, "Likewise to you, sir." He kept on with his intimidation approach—oh, I mean his pretended assessment. "This is a complicated place for a female," he scoffed. Unyielding, I replied, "I'm realizing that more and more each day, sir." He slowly nodded his head and walked away.

After catching my breath, I must say, that was a pivotal moment in my career as a female corrections officer. I was Courageous Cat (for those who remember the cartoon), at that moment of passionate uncertainty. I didn't know what to expect. I didn't know what he expected, and I didn't care. But, if I had to bet on it, I would have betted that he was looking for a way to have me fired. It was apparent that he was pissed off. There is no doubt in my mind that I was not the first female he approached, nor was I the last. I feel sorrow and empathy for those who fell victim.

I continued to work but not without anticipating that he would plot to get rid of me somehow, sooner or later. The time finally came for the rookies to be appointed to their permanent positions in another prison—but not before meeting with him to obtain his approval. We were given three choices, and we had to choose one, but he had to approve of it. It was at this time that I was certain he would take the opportunity to terminate me since it was the end of the ninety-day probationary period. Once again, my courage was slowly creeping out the door. This time I had to face him alone. I didn't have a choice in the matter, and it was something that had to be done—that's if, I wanted to move forward as a corrections officer.

On that day, we all waited outside of his office to be called in, one by one. When he called my name, I cringed. I inched my way into his office. There he was, pompously sitting at his desk with his arms folded across his big, fat, sloppy belly. I would not allow him to address me first. I figured I would be the aggressor and make the first move. (Here we go, back to the chess game again.) So, I jumped right into it. Before he could even open his mouth, I said, "I've chosen to go to a correctional facility for women. I believe working with females would be more conducive for me." Then I attempted to hand him my assignment papers. He looked at me, paused, and slowly reached for the paperwork while trying to touch my hand. I slightly pulled back and placed the paperwork on his desk. He then took forever and a day, gawking at the one piece of paper that required his signature. Without saying a word, I just stood there waiting patiently. He finally checked off his approval.

Slowly he raised his hand to return the paperwork to me,

attempting once again to touch my hand. I continued to stand there with my hands behind by back. Then he threw the papers on his desk and said in a condescending manner, "I approve of you." I was tempted to snatch the papers off his desk and tell him to go take a long-ass walk on a short-ass pier. I just wanted to get away from him. Thank goodness, I was able to hold my temper. I quickly retrieved the papers from his desk and reluctantly extended my gratitude. I refused to stoop to his level. With his incredibly snobbish attitude, he replied, "Yeah, yeah. Whatever." I never looked back and kept walking toward the door to a better and more familiar environment, and that was working with females.

I never heard from or saw him again. However, before my assignment was etched in stone, I was confronted once again with yet another inopportune episode that would put my position as a corrections officer, and potentially my freedom, in jeopardy. Simply put, the adversary was a bitter man, my ex-husband. By this time, we were officially divorced. I mentioned earlier that he was a county prosecutor. Unfortunately, he was a very spiteful human being, which was one of the primary reasons we parted ways—in addition to my misfortune that he was physically abusive. To add to his anger, he was furious that I had gone into law enforcement. It just so happened that during our divorce proceedings, the DOC informed me that they were testing after being on their waiting list for several years. On several occasions he threatened that his main objective was to have me terminated. He vowed that he was not going to stop until it happened.

Which brings me to this point. A couple of days before starting my new assignment at the correctional facility for women, he called the chief and claimed that I had threatened him with a gun—a serious allegation for anyone, let alone an officer of the law. I could hardly catch my breath before there was something else happening to me. My on-the-job training had involved exclusively male officials and their illegal misconduct or illicit behavior. This time, I am honored to say that the captain, whom I had been skeptical about, had the allegations thoroughly investigated.

My ex-husband, as I mentioned, was an attorney. He did not have a good reputation inside the law enforcement world. Therefore, his credibility was in question right from the door. I received a courtesy call from the captain informing that the DOC's investigation proved his allegations had no merit, and as a result, they dismissed the case. I was totally unaware of my ex's allegations until that very moment. This was due to the captain's intervention and control over the entire investigation. Be that as it may, I was not surprised to find out that my ex was not charged with filing a false police report. On the other hand, being the disgruntled man that he was, he still was not satisfied and continued to harass me until I filed a permanent restraining order. In due course, his lies and deceitful ways backfired. Eventually, he lost his license to practice law, which inevitably destroyed his career. I continued to move forward without incident, from him anyway, and began my new assignment working in a female correctional facility.

THE CONTRAST

THE CORRECTIONAL FACILITY FOR WOMEN was a total contrast to the men's prison. I was taken by surprise when I noticed the female prisoners casually walking along an open grassy area. When I pulled into the prison grounds, I was looking around for gates or fences, but I didn't see any. This reflected the different levels of security structured by the DOC. This area of the institution was identified as the minimum security section, which I later realized was the reason behind the fenceless perimeters. The prisoners in this area were considered nonviolent with less than a year remaining before released. Supposedly, they posed no threat to the public, so this was the least restricted area of the prison. I still consider that too liberal.

I was so accustomed to the training in a maximum security prison that I almost forgot about the different levels of security until I saw the prisoners walking about so freely. Driving up to the main office was more like driving on a college campus. I parked and walked inside where I presented my ID badge and signed the logbook. An officer informed me that I was parked in the wrong area and directed me to the personnel parking lot. While looking for another parking space, I observed the prisoners more closely as they leisurely strolled along. I could not believe what I was seeing. If I had not known that I was on the grounds of a female correctional facility, I would have thought that it was a coed correctional facility. Some of the prisoners looked like heterosexual couples. I couldn't help but notice the great measures some of the females were allowed to alter their appearances in order to emulate a man, due to their sexual preferences. For instance, some had bald heads and facial hair. During that time, street clothes and shoes were permissible, which gave them the option of wearing men's attire. One would think that would be prohibited for a litany of reasons, since such eye-catching changes could be considered disguises and result in a serious breach of security. (Today prisoners are issued uniform state prison clothes and shoes.) I am sure I was not the only one doing a double take when approaching the grounds of this particular female institution.

In any event, the option to transfer to a female facility was a great relief for me. I imagined that it would be ideal working among my own species, so to speak, assuming I would be more apt to relate to the female prisoners—the so-called softer side of prison. Anyway, it sounded logical. Once again I was dead wrong. These were no bunnies behind bars. Many of them had an imposing presence. You could say that I was blindsided by my own misconception or ignorance, believing that it would be a cakewalk for me, as a female, to deal with other females. The conglomerate of catfights, quarrelsome lovers, endless crying, backbiting, and, last but not least, the mood swings and temper tantrums were without end. In addition, a great number of the females were physically abusing their lovers, and jealousy ran rampant. Whether it was because her partner was admiring or talking to another prisoner, or because she was a little too chummy with one of the officers, male or female, it did not matter. Jealousy was their main gripe and the root of the majority of their bouts.

The females were much more argumentative than the men and made constant verbal threats. The women were definitely more emotionally driven than the men. Their issues stemmed from their ongoing, overtly intimate relationships. There was little to no crying or bickering among the male prisoners. When I worked the overnight shift in the male prison, every so often I would hear faint sounds of whimpering during my late-night inspections, similar to a child calling for their mother in the middle of the night. These muffled cries were coming from the depths of a dark cell of a hardened male criminal. Be that as it may, there was no comparison when it came to the fighting among the men.

When the men fought, it was an animalistic brawl. At times, the fights were deadly enough to put the entire institution on lockdown. Ending up lots of times in death and destruction, especially if the fight started outside in the yard, where hundreds of prisoners gathered at one time. The huge yard simulated a coliseum where the men would brawl like gladiators. Too often, they were armed with makeshift weapons, better known as "shanks". Somehow, they would conceal the shanks—even though the prisoners were searched before entering the yard—to maim and kill, making every effort to fight to the death.

For obvious reasons, officers were not posted in the yard. Occasionally, an officer in the tower would have to fire off several rounds of gunfire into the air, ordering the prisoners to stop fighting, or they would be shot. On other occasions, an Emergency Response Team (ERT) would suit up in riot gear and go into the yard to seize the fight. All officers were trained for these emergency situations. Therefore, you'd better be ready if you were called. There were times when the warden simply let the prisoners fight until they tired themselves out, and then the officers would ambush the yard to make the necessary arrests. New technology and money has allowed surveillance cameras in the yards, assisting the department in pinpointing the perpetrators.

Speaking of emergency teams, there is another team known as the Cell Extraction Team (CET). In this situation, five officers suit up in riot gear and forcibly remove a defiant prisoner who refuses to come out of a cell. At the same time, there is a supervising officer videotaping the entire process in order to capture anything that may go wrong, protecting the rights of both the officer and the prisoner. Once the prisoner has been seized, he is immediately placed into solitary confinement, better known as the hole. This is protocol after any physical altercation. The hole is another level of punishment, in which prisoners are on lockdown for twenty-three hours of the day. Then they are released from a triple-locked cell for one hour to shower and go outside for some fresh air. From there, they are moved into a small cage, where they are guarded by two officers. After that one hour, they are escorted back to their cell for twenty-three more hours. By the way, the same disciplinary actions are imposed on the females.

With respect to physical fights between the females, the situation was quite different. Their yard was significantly smaller, where officers were always posted in the yard. Their fights were nowhere near as violent and vicious as the men. There were many physical or verbal altercations during which officers, including myself, would intercede as the voice of reason, with minimal difficulty. This would pretty much bring the volatile situation to a truce. And, I would like to say, afterward there were plenty of times when we could readily have a meaningful woman-to-woman conversation. Any attempt to be the voice of reason during a physical altercation between the men was highly unlikely, especially coming from a female officer.

I almost made that fatal mistake early in my career wherein, I nearly suffered the consequences of a razor-blade-slinging prisoner. Just in case you forgot, I spoke about how the prisoners were permitted to purchase razor blades from the inmate commissary for shaving, which is a problematic situation, as razor blades are also used to maim other prisoners and officers. The razor blade episode quickly taught me to always proceed with caution because any situation can become deadly. I had no problem stepping back and allowing the heroes to take over. My main objective as a corrections officer was to go home at the end of my shift, alive and well.

While there were opportunities to engage in lengthy conversations with the female prisoners, unquestionably there was a difference when it came to lengthy conversations with male prisoners. This is not to say that I didn't converse with the men. I just found it to be inappropriate. In all reality, I would say that most long, drawn-out conversations would be swayed by the male prisoner or became misleading. What I am trying to say, is that the conversation could be easily misconstrued as a prelude to sex or something else detrimental. This could very well be the same with the female prisoner since both prisoners have the propensity to manipulate the officer. In my view, conversing with a male prisoner too often can be misinterpreted, not only by the prisoner, but also by other prisoners and officers, particularly those seeking to cause trouble. I've said this before; I'm convinced that an officer's reputation and respect carries credence much greater than their badge.

In conversing with a female prisoner, I could relate to her perhaps as a daughter, a sister, or even a mother, invariably mindful of the reality that she was still a convicted criminal. I was certainly able to identify with some of the women on the level of being raised in a downtrodden city. For instance, becoming a mother as a teenager and living in the city projects among some of the worst criminals, whom I grew up with and knew personally. So many of the female prisoners were victims of child molestation, sexual abuse, and domestic violence that, in turn, linked them to their mishaps. The same concept relates to the male prisoner. However, I was more empathetic when listening woman to woman about a female's dilemmas and hardships. To this day, I have visible and emotional scars from the domestic abuse I endured, so I understood.

As terrible as that sounds, it is minuscule compared to some of their adversities that led them to even greater trials and tribulations. I consider myself truly blessed to be where I am today, mentally and physically. By no means do I take this life for granted. How incongruous, that I escaped the violence of the prison world with no scars, but I was unable to escape the scars of domestic violence by a loved one in the comfort and security of my own home. The irony of it all, was that the person responsible was my ex-husband, an attorney who prided himself on upholding the law. These are some of the reasons that I easily identified with many of the females and their plights. I can never forget where I came from. There is no escaping the mirrors that have propelled me to humility and self-confidence. I pray that during my career as a corrections officer, I was able to uplift a prisoner to envision the brighter side of life.

Looking at things from that standpoint, it was rewarding to work with the female prisoners. Conversely, this female correctional institution was openly inundated with homosexuality. With all due respect, I am not passing judgment on anyone's sexual preference. I merely could not comprehend the overly aggressive persuasion that some of the lesbians imposed on the other females. No matter how uninterested another female made it known—whether she was heterosexual, bisexual, or homosexual—some lesbians were so antagonistic that they would instigate a physical fight upon rejection.

Regarding homosexuality among male prisoners, well, that word, in and of itself, was taboo. The subject matter for all intents and purposes was OTDL, "On The Down Low." This suggests that a man is secretly having sex with another man. My personal interpretation of the DL is "Double Life" because these men are not only having sex with each other, but they also were living a double life by having sex with their heterosexual partner, who believes that they are in a heterosexual relationship. Therefore, the expression should be "A Double Life on the Down Low." These men may, or may not, divulge their sexual improprieties to their male partner, who could very well be exclusively, homosexual. What's even more peculiar, a lot of these men do not consider their sexual behavior with the same sex as homosexuality. It's simply referred to as "jail sex." During their undercover behavior, they solicit each other secretively, with special codes or signals while in prison and on the streets.

Let me be clear about this. There are overt homosexuals or gay men in prison as well. Flamers, fags, fagits, and maletails are just a few of the terms that they are sometimes labeled. They have no problem flaunting their sexual preferences and wants. They purposely brand themselves with their very flamboyant behavior, which stands out loud and proud in the crowd. They parade around the prisons strutting their stuff like prostitutes on a Las Vegas strip. Some wear cutoff halter shirts, extremely tight pants, makeup and nail polish to emulate a woman as much as possible.

Not to mention their stylish hairdos. At the same time, mincing no words about what they want and what they will do to get it. Otherwise, homosexuality in the male prison is not a topic for discussion. Although, it is another story when the lights go out at night and the sexual secrecies rear their heads—and I mean that in every sense of the word. The sexual escapades commence inside of their dark, six-by-eight-foot dark cells all through the night. Unless they are caught in the act— and it happens more often than not—no one will ever know who's zoomin' who, as we used to say, including their heterosexual significant others, their wives and girlfriends who visit them religiously. In most cases, these women are ignorant to the facts or turn a blind eye. They have a tendency or simply want to believe that just because their husband or boyfriend is incarcerated, solely with men, that they have a monogamous, quintessential relationship.

There are institutions in the country exclusively for male pedophiles, open homosexuals and men who have been convicted for heinous sex crimes. The main reason for this separation is that the sexual predators are not well received sometimes, by the men in other prisons. Therefore, they are alienated for their own safety in an attempt to keep them out of harm's way. Except for the fact, that it is practically impossible to house them all in one place, indicative of my previous accounts regarding their presence in a standard male prison.

Now there are male and female prisoners who secretly carried out their homosexual escapades the entire time they were incarcerated, supposedly unbeknownst to anyone. While locked up, people did whatever it took to satisfy their libido. However, upon being released, they resorted to their heterosexual way of living. Irrespective of what I have expressed pertaining to their sexual behaviors, there were plenty of circumstances that were beyond their control, and many prisoners were brutally raped repeatedly by other prisoners and corrections officers. There were others who engaged in sexual bartering or coercion.

There are so many reasons for their sexual dealings, and the situation exists in all prisons. Still, most male prisoners will emphatically deny their sexual encounters, in contrast to most female prisoners, who have no shame in their game and no problem displaying their affection. After all, sex is a basic human instinct, whether you are locked up inside behind the wall or exercising your free will living on the outside.

FEMININE NATURE

HOMOSEXUALITY IN THIS FEMALE CORRECTIONAL facility was vastly aggressive and widely displayed among the prisoners, as well as the female officers. I found myself embroiled in repetitive battles, resisting the insistent and unfriendly propositions of overzealous lesbians. Some were so hard-pressed that they made it appear as though the female prison was a recruitment center for homosexuality. No disrespect intended. Actually, I would compare some of their measures to a gang initiation. They made it seem like it was a do-or-die situation just to see how many heterosexual females they could convert, if that's the proper word to use.

It sounds a bit exaggerated, but this particular group of women I am referring to portrayed themselves as desperate, and they did whatever it took to enforce their personal beliefs. The in-your-face confrontations that the heterosexual females had to contend with were excessive and unprovoked. They were determined to get what they wanted, even when it became obvious that they were being insulting and offensive. Every time I turned around, I was defending my heterosexuality or otherwise, be stripped of my feminine nature, so it seemed. The awkwardness of it all was very unsettling, largely because they were so pushy. I was so ready to get the hell up out of there. I felt like I had jumped from the frying pan into the fire, for making the decision to leave the male prison to go there.

Almost immediately, I determined that I had made yet, another mistake, and I would have been better off working in a male institution. At least, as a woman, I was accustomed to a man's flirtatious ways. Sexual overtures coming from another woman, and in such an antagonistic manner, were something I was not about to get used to or put up with. Here I was again, mentally struggling to hold on to this position as a corrections officer. Some of the lesbian prisoners had such a lack of respect for the female officers, and were so belligerent, that our constant face-to-face encounters would surely end up in a physical altercation.

I hadn't been there for a good two weeks before I was already requesting a transfer. I figured with the lateral transfers still in effect, the sooner I informed them of my decision, the sooner I could transfer to another institution, preferably for men. This is when the chief, as she preferred to be called, became highly agitated when I candidly conveyed my frustrations and asked for a transfer. "Why so soon?" she asked. "Are you ill at ease with the presence of so many lesbians?" I assumed that she had a notion; therefore, I responded with the truth. "With all due respect for the right to choose and homosexuality, it's not their presence, per se; it's those with the belligerent attitudes that are so bothersome."

She simply said, "I understand how you feel. I'll see what I can do." Her body language and actions gave a different impression.

From that moment on, I felt as though I had walked right into a collision course. I only voiced my opinion because she asked. I was inclined to believe that she was offended by my candor because she was a lesbian herself, as she deemed necessary to disclose. "Did you know that I am a lesbian?" I honestly didn't understand the relevancy in her statement or why she felt the need to divulge her sexuality. Additionally, I didn't know where she was going with the conversation. I was surprised at her mannerism and her professionalism. I was puzzled when I responded, "I had no idea. I hope you weren't offended by my comments." Without answering my question, she told me that I could be excused, and she would work on my transfer. Nevertheless, it was quite evident that she was offended by my I-couldn't-care-less attitude when she intercepted my transfer request for no apparent reason. She continued to show her animosity from that point on by abusing her authority.

She really got my attention when she began to assign me job details that obligated me to remain on post well past my shift that ended at 10:00 p.m. This was considered mandatory overtime, according to DOC policies and procedures. By definition, mandatory overtime is an essential part of a corrections officer's job description; however, not for consecutive weeks at a time unless, of course, the entire institution was on an emergency lockdown. Otherwise, all job details were supposed to be delegated on a rotation basis—most importantly, mandatory overtime. The extra money on payday was gratifying, but I was bone-tired at the end of the week.

I didn't want to exhibit the slightest hint of insubordination and subject myself to a reprimand. Consequently, I had to be patient and roll with the punches, for lack of a better term. Her abuse of power, associated with her inflated ego, went on for weeks, causing me to get home in the wee hours of the morning, sometimes just before the break of day. The domino effect of fatigue—associated with commuting for over an hour, suffering from a lack of sleep, and then getting right back up to narrowly make it to 2:00 p.m. lineup—was wearing me out. Reflecting all the while that I had made the sacrifice to take this long commute because I believed working in a female correctional facility would be a better environment for me. She made her bitterness crystal clear during the routine lineups, when she went out of her way to ridicule me in the presence of the other officers by seeking out unimportant flaws in my appearance or uniform. She was an unlikable person to begin with, as she pushed her way around the prison. In my opinion, she went to extreme measures to ensure that the female officers were stripped completely of their feminine nature. Jewelry and makeup of any kind were prohibited, including clear lip gloss. Our nails had to be cut short, as close to the finger as possible, and absolutely no nail polish could be worn, including clear polish. God forbid if we wore perfume or fragrance-based lotions of any kind. She was audacious enough to lean in close and smell females during lineup. You read it right. She would actually walk up to a female officer and sniff her as if she was a dog in heat. It was unbelievable! If a female officer had shoulder-length hair, it had to be pulled up and pinned; ponytails were unacceptable. She insisted that females cut their hair short enough so it would not touch the collar of their uniforms.

Moreover, she was uncompromising when enforcing specific rules and regulations implemented by her, and not by the DOC. One would get the impression that we were on a military base. I thought her next move would be to administer crew cuts for the females. My patience began to wear thin, dealing with the ongoing issues of her drunk-with-power disposition. Eventually,

I had no other choice but to go over her head and reach out to the commissioner. Without her knowledge, I wrote him a certified letter of hardship requesting a transfer. I suggested that my immediate concern was the well-being of my children, and I needed to be closer to home. Never once did I allude to the fact that I was in the midst of utter chaos and the chief was riding my coattail. I left that alone. I did not want to show any dissension with respect to her decision to intercept my initial transfer request. I left that open for her to explain.

Sure enough, he approved my transfer, no questions asked, and that did not sit well with her at all. First of all, I went behind her back and over her head. She could not refute the commissioner's decision though. Unfortunately, she used her position to take advantage of the situation by using all sorts of tactics to delay the transfer. It did not affect me much at first because I knew the transfer was definitely approved. She could not delay it forever. To my dismay, it felt like forever, given that I ended up working there for almost two years, largely due to her vindictiveness. She continuously made pleas to the commissioner regarding the lack of officers.

Her favorite rhetoric was "More female officers were in demand because too many of the female prisoners were being mistreated and sexually assaulted by the male officers." There was some validity to that statement, which led to ongoing investigations. However, Internal Affairs discovered that the mistreatment and sexual abuse stemmed from, more than anyone else, the female prisoners and the female officers. She conveniently left out the oppressive treatment by the prisoner towards her lesbian partner, which was out of control. The male officers were simply being singled out and scrutinized under a larger microscope because they were men. Thus, some of these happenings legitimately delayed my transfer. Simply speaking, and in spite of everything that was going on, her major objective was to get rid of the male officers and hire all female officers.

There were significantly more female officers there as opposed to the female officers in the male prisons. She sought after any excuse to have the prison overseen by primarily women, and she had no problem in conveying this to administration and anyone else who would listen. Fortunately, she did not have the control she feigned. In due course, her false reasoning to delay my transfer was regarded invalid. After coming under suspicion for other violations, her abuse of authority was revealed, and she was eventually demoted.

After much persistence, the commissioner finally appointed me to another institution much closer to my home. It also happened to be one of the most notorious prisons for men in the country. Looking back, I ended up working with the female prisoners for much longer than I anticipated, and during that time, I had to strategically toil my way through the homosexual aggression from both prisoners and officers, not to mention the chief. It took me some time to learn how to respond as a professional officer, rather than react to the prisoners' provoking methods. I believe that I often allowed myself to be pulled out of character because it was a woman-to-woman encounter. There were many times that I was ready and willing to engage in a fistfight. I would never bait a man into a physical altercation. Still, that was not an excuse.

I will admit those were challenging times for me; working in a female correctional facility, they were also times of growing and learning how to be a competent corrections officer. I do feel as though I learned a lot, specifically humility and patience in such a volatile, unstable environment. The sexual overtures were still relentless. I simply learned how to handle myself better and ignore ignorance. The following phrase almost became a slogan for me because I found myself repeating it: "I love being a woman, I love being with a man, and, most of all, I love the penetration of a man." I know it is a little vulgar, but prison is a vulgar place. If I could have paraded around holding up those words on a banner, I certainly would have done so. That is how often I had to repeat myself.

Too often, my peacekeeping methods did not matter. Those were the times I tried to be a bit lighthearted in an attempt to break the ice, believing that I could get some of them to loosen up a little. A few would laugh, and we would laugh together. (All things considered, we still had to learn how to coexist with one another.) Nonetheless, you had the naysayers who did not find anything funny. They were the loudmouthed bullies who dared to get in my face and challenge me on my sexual origin, which I found to be absurd. In essence, just plain old troublemakers who made it bad for others and this is where I drew the line.

I pointed out, with conviction, what I considered to be the cold hard facts, solely directed at them. "From one woman to another, your ineffective, so-called manly aggressions don't faze me. We were born with the same anatomy, we use the same bathrooms, and you are not intimidating. So back the fuck up!" Ill feelings like this, I never wanted to display. However, every so often I had to teeter along the boundaries of a stone-cold bitch to assert my position of authority. After all, we were in a prison, and I was a corrections officer. Regardless, it was not my position to reach for the handcuffs or go into bitch mode every time something was said that I did not agree with. Every now and then, I had to let them know that I came from some of the same places they did and I understood some of their misplaced anger. Then, with self-assurance, I ordered them to take it down because I could be a bitch too.

When things were levelheaded, I would let them know I had the right to choose, just as they did, and I chose to stay out of jail and to exercise my right as a heterosexual. It all boiled down to respecting one another. On top of that, the last thing I wanted to do was show fear. In some of our girly conversations, if-you-will, it didn't matter that the prisoner was a lesbian; "she" was still a female, innate with her feminine nature, and that would be the gist of our discussions as women. It was for those reasons that I became more compassionate with the female prisoners—although never complacent. They were still convicted criminals. Whether they were guilty or innocent was not for me to say. For whatever reasons, it was only those chosen few who were constantly revved up with hostility. To that end, it was not my intent to sound homophobic; or as though I was generalizing the lesbian prisoners as all having a fierce dispositions; or to pass judgment in any way, form or fashion.

THE ABYSS

AFTER I CONSIDERED VARIOUS CHOICES, it did not matter whether this transfer was the right choice; it was a necessary one. I could not wait to get away from the endless bullying and cattiness between the women in the female correctional facility. The last thing I wanted to do was jeopardize my career because of a physical altercation with another grown woman. Here I was, running once again. All the same, making this decision did come with its pros and cons. On one hand, it cut my commute time in half and enabled me to be closer to my children. On the other hand, this same prison was infamously known as the bottomless pit or the abyss.

Clearly I had never entered a lion's den, but the sights and sounds resembled those I had heard and seen on the big screen. Right from the door, the prison was noticeably different from the two male prisons I had ventured into during my orientation and probationary period. It diminished the female prison to the likings of an elementary school. The strange, loud noises sounded liked confusion and disorder. They were especially frightening when echoing throughout the prison. It was one of the largest prisons in the country, housing twenty-five hundred prisoners. It was secured by approximately, 800 corrections officers, of which, 50 were women.

Since I had requested this lateral transfer, I was the only rookie to start this new assignment. Usually new rookies came in groups; therefore, my new experience was even worse, given that I did not have anyone with whom to share my fears. Even though I had been working for nearly three years by then, a newcomer was always considered a rookie, and technically I was because every prison is different. Yet it was evident that some things remained the same. For one, the female corrections officers were their usual standoffish selves. They would intentionally bypass me without any verbal communication, and they displayed a reluctance to assist me in learning new job details. Regrettably, this type of behavior among female officers was prevalent. This was a disservice to ourselves particularly when you take into account the vastness of the male prison and that we were the extreme minority. I went there with the preconceived notion that the females must have formed a much better alliance for that very reason. It was simply another lapse in my judgment.

I must say—I was taken aback upon learning how divided the females were because in the female correctional facility, the male officers were the minority, but for some strange reason, the females were still at each other's throats. It was problematic and awfully disappointing, to say the least. On the whole, this simply gave the men an even greater advantage over the female officers because of the blatant dissention going on between us.

Meanwhile the men had nothing else better to do, but observe and take notes for future underhandedness. For now, the men, officers and prisoners, were jumping through hoops to make a good impression. As I pointed out earlier, this was typical when any new female landed on the scene, which implied nine out of ten times that there was an ulterior motive behind their hospitable mannerisms.

My first directive was to stand post in the central point of the prison and wait for another officer to escort me to the warden's office for a briefing. It happened to be lunchtime, and the prisoners were being called, tier by tier, to make their way to the mess hall. Therefore, I had to stand post in the middle of this mass movement. There were hundreds of prisoners moving about without restraints. While standing there with a measly ten officers, all men, and lacking knowledge of the protocol, I got the distinct impression that I was purposely put there for display so that the men could observe—and feel—the presence of a new female officer. I described this to you earlier. You know, new females bring about fresh new meat.

I stood there feeling like a puppy stranded in the heart of the Sahara Desert. The intensity of the heat was stifling behind the thick concrete walls, with air conditioners located in the business offices only. At last, after what seemed like an eternity, a female officer emerged to inform me that she was going to escort me to the warden's office. Then, without warning, she dashed ahead of me as if I knew where to go. After several steps, I was compelled to suggest that she slow down so that I could keep up. I am sure she expected me to run behind her, but that was not going to happen.

It is rather tedious drawing attention to the discord between the females. But, then again, I want it understood that it was a created tension that resonated throughout the department. It was pointless and did nothing but discredit the female officers in the end. Sadly, the bone of contention was an accumulation of jealousy and competing for the attention of the men, whether it was an officer or a prisoner. The men, in the meantime, were either competing among themselves or enjoying the catfights. It was similar to rivalries between students in high school and college. Point in case, once the female officer and I got closer to the warden's office, she callously pointed to his door, showing no courtesy whatsoever, and kept walking without saying one word. I was so used to females' ornery ways that I just walked inside.

I was impressed that the warden immediately stood up like a gentleman, shook my hand, and introduced himself. Chivalry was definitely something I was not accustomed to in the DOC. Oftentimes, the men would treat and address the women as if they were men, and without any qualms, they would pretend we weren't even present in the room by reiterating, "Females have no place behind the wall." For the duration of the warden's briefing, a female lieutenant was present, weirdly pretending to be preoccupied. She never spoke and avoided making eye contact during the entire briefing. She simply hovered around the warden as if she was his personal bodyguard. In the meantime, he went over the policies and procedures of the institution. When he began to wrap things up and proceeded to the door to take me on a tour of the prison, he finally acknowledged her and formerly introduced us. I know, I said something about his chivalry; evidently I spoke too soon.

"Oh, I almost forgot," he proclaimed, with a cunning look in his eyes, feigning as if he had forgotten that she was even in the room. "She's the only female lieutenant working here on second shift." Then she looked me in the eyes and slightly bowed her head, saying nothing. I returned the gesture. Precisely as he and I were exiting the room, she said, "I hope you can handle yourself in the abyss." Offhandedly, I responded, "I don't understand what you mean." Swiftly and cynically, she shot back, "This is not a place for women." I came back just as swift and just as cynical. "I'm confused. I thought the warden said that you are employed here as a lieutenant?" Sarcastically she replied, "But I can handle myself!" My reaction was contemptuous. "Really, that's good to know and an implication that I should have no problem. Please try to enjoy the rest of your day because I plan to enjoy mine." That ended our spiteful spat, then the warden opened the door.

I was irate when I turned away with my so-called tough face on, heading out the door. I was highly disappointed in my conduct. I could not believe that I walked right into that collision course of exchanging words. I thought that I had conquered that hurdle when I left the female correctional institution. Apparently I was harboring some resentment and left myself wide open for that childish type of scene that played out right in front of the warden, who evidently got a kick out of it. I must confess, though, I was flat out intimidated by the whole range of things and let my guard down. Instead of her welcoming me on board, and providing some support from one woman to another, she made it her business to further invoke fear.

Looking at it another way, it was a good thing that I had my so-called game face on because the warden and I walked right smack into another busy mass movement. Subsequent to the lieutenant's inflammatory remarks, my fears magnified, and I started to become increasingly unsure of myself. Could my psyche handle being locked inside of this massive prison, enclosed by thousands of the most notorious and dangerous criminal men in the country? It was a lot to take in.

Our first stop on the tour was the infamous hole. It was the most haunting experience ever. Truthfully, I do not remember too much after that because what I underwent is almost too inexplicable to put into words. It hurled a shadow over everything else that occurred that day. As far as upholding my customary game face, I was clueless to what that meant at that moment in time. First and foremost, I want you to bear in mind that this maximum security state institution was over one hundred years old with minimal upgrades. To begin the tour, we had to walk to the opposite side of the institution to retrieve the key for the hole from the central control room. Once we returned, the officer on duty was alerted over the radio that we were coming down for a tour.

I was shocked beyond measure to learn that the officer on duty did not have access to a key. The only keys in the officer's possession were the keys to the cell gates of the one hundred prisoners confined in the hole. How baffling is that? The officer had access to the keys for the prisoners to exit but didn't have access to the key for his own exit. The institution's logic behind this, in my opinion, was pure idiocy. In short, their line of reasoning was that the officer was not permitted to have the key because the prisoners could overpower him, take the key, let themselves out, and incite a riot. Regardless, there was no exit strategy for the lone officer.

To add to this idiotic situation, it took what appeared to be the pure muscle and strength of two men to open and close this huge, wide steel door. When the door finally slammed shut behind us, I shuddered. I immediately started gasping for air when we began to descend underground into the hole. This was not before the warden turned around and handed the key to another officer on the other side of the door, who then locked us inside and left with the key in hand. That's when things started to take a disturbing turn for me. It was as if we were entering a vault of burial chambers. Conveying to you the reality of this whole experience is mind-boggling. Envision walking into the house of horrors at an amusement park, only this was not amusing, and it was not staged. Or imagine the worst horror film that you have ever seen, and think about how it made you cringe, even though you knew it was fictitious. This was not fictitious. It was real, real to the core.

The feeling of revulsion caused me to quiver uncontrollably. Besides the fact that the hole was damp, dark, and cold, the combination of the stench and filth was like inhaling poisonous fumes. Each prisoner's cell had an uncanny resemblance to a tomb. "These are tombs for the dead, not cells for the living," I muttered to myself. There were no windows and one old, dusty, dim lamp on the officer's filthy desk. I do not recall any other lighting. I'm sure there had to be some lighting; we were not in complete darkness, although that's how it came across to me. When we came upon the first tomb-like cell, the warden went into a spiel about one prisoner who had been living in this same cell for twenty-seven years.

By this time, I was breathless. I was making every effort to block out everything in my sight. Then I began to feel queasy and felt as if I was losing consciousness. It's bizarre trying to express what was happening, but having the presence of mind to stay focused, I would not allow myself to fall helplessly in such deplorable conditions. Therefore, I collected every ounce of strength that I had to maintain my balance. I was banking on the fact that we were on our way out of there. It was like being in the middle of a horrific nightmare and desperately needing someone to wake me. There was no question in my mind; at that point, that I was going to jump ship as soon as I got up for air. I viewed this as a total disregard for human life, and I was right in the center of it, trapped in the guts of the abyss. I couldn't even hide if I wanted to. While all of this was going on, I was desperately trying to adjust myself to this gloomy atmosphere and give my undivided attention to the warden, who was rambling on about the prisoners' horrendous living conditions. The story about the one prisoner who had lived in this atrocious hole for twenty-seven years was one that was going far beyond my intellectual capability. At that juncture, I don't think that I was coherent. I couldn't fathom being confined in such an uninhabitable place for twenty-seven seconds, let alone twenty-seven years! Most of the prisoners were languishing in their cells and appeared to be desiccated without life, like corpses, yet they were breathing. It was indescribable. Zombies was the only depiction I could think of when I attempted to look them in their faces, because I could not.

The feeling of being trapped like a wild beast became ever so real and frightening. The longer we were down there in what I considered to be a bottomless pit, the more difficult it became for me to concentrate and breathe. Without exaggerating, I was suffocating. It was the most chilling scene I had ever come across in my life. It was a far cry from unexpectedly walking up on an actual dead corpse lying in the alleyway or a hallway in the housing projects. I had seen more of that than I cared to remember. Up until that point, I thought that I had seen the worst of things, but nothing surpasses what I saw and experienced that day. To see death in the living and in utter disregard for human life is inexpressible. I can't make it clear enough how relieved I was when the warden asked me if I wanted to proceed with the tour. In a flash, I answered, "No, please, no. I've had enough." What I wanted to do was make a rapid beeline to the stairs and get back up to higher ground. At least I could breathe remotely better and see my hand in front of my face.

Once we were above ground, I gained a tad more composure, especially when he informed me that the female officers were not posted in the hole. "Reason being, there were more than enough male officers who volunteered to work there in order to stay out of the general population," he clarified. "These particular officers feel a sense of security in the hole, figuring if a riot was to break out, they would be out of harm's way." That statement was ambiguous to me. I was not going to ask him to elaborate. I didn't give a hoot as long as I did not have to work down there. Despite that, I knew I was standing in front of my most crucial life challenge by far, working in the abyss. This was certainly much greater than anything that I had been through previously involving the DOC.

To add to this difficult challenge, I was completely aware of the fact that I was a new fresh piece of meat being targeted by the predators—the prisoners and officers. No matter what, I had to prove to myself that I had confidence in my own merit, and that I could get through this incomparable test or submit my letter of resignation. Consequently, my primary focus remained on the state's lucrative salary and first-rate health care benefits. This was tremendously beneficial to my children and me. Keeping those essentials in mind, along with my tenacity, kept me afloat, as did the most obvious reason: staying alive. In spite of it all, before I knew it I was becoming acclimated to the prison's massiveness, so I began voluntarily working overtime.

During overtime one morning, I was posted on an easy job answering phones when I received a call from the warden. "So far, you seem to be catching on and working well," he stated. "Slowly, but surely," I replied. He then said, "If you have any questions, don't hesitate to ask." I graciously replied, "Thank you, sir." I took for granted that ended our conversation, but that was not the case. He had something else to say. "Oh, I also wanted to let you know that you are receiving quite a few compliments." I paused at first and then said, "Compliments?" My reaction was one of uneasiness—the same uncomfortable sentiment I felt when I was a rookie and received that unwarranted call from the deputy warden. Usually my intuition served me right, and the vibe I was getting right then from the warden was totally off base. The more I worked with the officers, the more I began to recognize their slick and indirect methods. Until he said, "Okay, ten-four, I'm out." Without delay I responded, "Ten-four," and hung up the phone. "Okay," I said to myself, "take a chill pill girl, and get over yourself."

Before I could finish scolding myself, the phone rang, and it was the warden again. This time he made known what he really wanted to say when he called the first time. "I just need to ask you a question," he said. "Do you date men outside of your race?" Staggered, I replied, "What kind of question is that?" He casually answered, "Well, you should think about it. I'll call you back ten-four." Offering no explanation, he abruptly ended the call by hanging up. Once again, sexism was on autopilot for a lot of the men. And I'll repeat, I did not have those problems with the prisoners. Anyway, he called back a few hours later. "Well, did you think about it?" I rejected his off-the-wall pitch by letting him know that I didn't date law enforcement officers. I totally dismissed him and his question pertaining to the ethnicity of men I dated. It was none of his business. The boldness that they brandished was astounding. My thoughts, here we go again. Let me adjust my seat belt."

VISITS

VISITS ARE THE CRUX OF the prisons. There is a vast distinction between male and female prisoners with respect to their visit programs and their visitors. Hands down, there was no comparison between visits for the female prisoners and those of the male prisoners. I could never understand why the women were not permitted to receive regular visits as often as the men, especially from their children.

The prisoners in the female correctional facility were only permitted a one-hour visit per week, and the visitors were limited to two adults and one child. There were no exceptions to this rule. If the prisoner was the mother of more than one child, each child would have to visit on a separate visit day. Visit day for the female prisoners was in a controlled and restricted environment. It was very quiet and very short, and more importantly, very little presence of visitors. It was also a sad and depressing day that vibrated throughout the institution.

A great number of the female prisoners would hesitantly prepare for a visit, suspecting that it would end up in disappointment because their loved ones had failed to show so many times before. This was common practice on their visit day. Their typical visitors were grandparents, parents, and maybe a guardian, from time to time escorting their children. Every so often, they would receive a visit from their significant others, be it their husbands, boyfriends or partners. They would mosey in sporadically, often late, leaving her with only a few minutes of their time. Many of the females have expressed that that was their main reason for resorting to homosexuality during their incarceration. Everyone wants to be loved. Some gave way to that style of life, others were bisexual, while others resorted back to heterosexuality once they were released from prison.

All prisoners were subjected to a completely nude body search before and after a visit. During the process of this search, they had to open their mouths, lift up their tongues, squat down, bend over, spread their butt cheeks and cough to make sure they were not concealing anything between their buttocks. That's just the basics, along with a pat-down, searching their clothing, shoes and hair. This process took time away from the allotted hour for their visit, particularly when they weren't prepared in the first place.

The actual visit for the females took place in what seemed like a large classroom setting, that held approximately seventy-five to one hundred people. The layout was simply folding tables and chairs. The code of behavior for the visitor and the prisoner upon entering the visit area was a quick kiss on the cheek and a short embrace. Under no circumstances would there be any additional kissing on the lips or touching of any kind from that point on, or the visit would be instantly terminated. Once the visitor arrived, an officer escorted them to a designated seating area, where the prisoner sat on one side of the table and the visitor and one child sat on the other side. If the child left their seat to sit with their mother (the prisoner), it was the officer's responsibility to give the prisoner one warning: if the child left their seat again, the visit would be terminated. As the visits ended, they were permitted to repeat the one kiss on the cheek and a short embrace. For the most part, that was the extent of the visit program for the female prisoners.

Before I go into how immeasurably different the male prisoners' visit program was from the females', I want to pause here to express my viewpoint. The visit programs were as different as night and day. The female correctional facility was overbearing, stern and adhered to all rules. I couldn't figure it out. With the female prisoners, it was uncompromising; with the male prisoners, it was leniency. To add to the female prisoners' anguish were the distressing facts that they were not only being sexually assaulted frequently, and physically abused by their lesbian lovers, but they also were encountering the same immoral treatment from the male and female officers and civilian employees. Therefore, the department's feeble attempts to strictly monitor the females and their visits had no merit. I just wanted to point that out because I can't understand why the department was so hard on the females.

Now, let me spell out how the visit program was operated for the male prisoners, which is a manuscript all its own. First, the men received regular visits as often as three to four times a week, counting weekends and window visits. (There was no such thing as a window visit for the female prisoners.) Please note that these window visits were an alternative for the male prisoner if he was on punishment—that is, if he received some sort of infraction or violation. Regardless of his behavior, he was still allowed to receive a visit. (One minor infraction by the female prisoner and her visits were squashed. Then she would have to make an appeal for reinstatement of her visits.) On visit days in the male institution, so many people were visiting at one time that one would think there were no limitations on how many people were allowed to visit. However, there was an ineffective policy in place. It read four adults and *no* limit on the number of children. I will repeat the latter: no limit on the number of children. At this point, I do not have to remind you about the number of adults permitted to visit the female prisoners and especially, the number of children.

Please pay close attention to this next statement. When registering the visitors for the male prisoners, there were men and women, accompanied by young girls longing for a chance to be acquainted with a hot-blooded prisoner. What happens at that point, the prisoner would put her name on his visit list, or another thirsty prisoner's list. This type of activity was acceptable as long as she was not caught in a lie and could prove that she was eighteen years old, by presenting a photo ID (in most cases, a student ID). Many of the young girls were scarcely out of high school; therefore, only a few possessed a valid driver's license—that's if it wasn't counterfeit. The officers thoroughly scrutinized their IDs, considering that at least half of the young girls brought bogus ones because many of them were underage. This whole process can be perceived as sex trafficking.

The visit program for the men was a tragic set of circumstances in every aspect. Strange as it sounds, it was full of fairy-tale princesses in search of a knight. Why in the bowels of a prison's dungeon? I will never understand. The young girl's fabricated stories were endless pertaining to their relationship to the prisoner in an effort to become a permanent fixture in the visit center. The superior officers seemed to be unfazed by it all. They were aware of what was happening; however, they allowed it to grow out of control and turned a deaf ear in order to please the male prisoners. It was a constant reminder that this was indeed a man's world. As co-conspirators, the prisoners and the visitors had their lies sealed tight. In turn, these young women would return to the visit center, dragging along more young girls—or young prey, if you will—as fresh new meat. This ongoing cycle of showcasing was a continuous public display, as they utilized the visit center as a platform to solicit sex of underage girls, while also, promoting prostitution. Simply put, it was another one of the multitudes of crimes that are initiated and uninterrupted from behind the wall.

As time would have it, some of the same young girls would bring their newborn infants into the visit center that were, in fact, conceived right there on the grounds of the institution. Those uninhibited details are forthcoming. Nonetheless, there is something known as conjugal visits. If you did not know, a conjugal visit is when a prisoner and his "legal" wife are given complete privacy. Depending on the state prison and its policies, that privacy could last as long as twenty-four hours, thereby, allowing them to engage in unprotected sex. However, allow me to be clear and direct: conjugal visits were illegal in this state and illegal in most states throughout the country.

Anyway, visit days in this male prison produced crowds of people, mostly women and children, who stood in lines that wrapped around the outside perimeters of the prison. They would stand out there for hours at a time. The visit was scheduled for three hours, which would extend to almost four hours. This was mainly due to the draining process of trying to get the prisoners and their visitors to cooperate and vacate the visit center in a timely and orderly fashion. (Of course, I do not have to remind you of the time allotted for the female prisoners' visit.) Inclement weather conditions had no impact on the mass number of women who came in droves by any means necessary, including charter buses. In fact, some women walked to the prison from long distances and subsequently stood outside in line for hours, with their infants and children, until the doors of the registration office opened.

Let me give you a picture of what I am trying to demonstrate. When I arrived for duty at five o'clock in the morning, the visitors were already forming a line at the registration office, which opened five hours later at ten o'clock. The way that the women stood outside, patiently waiting for hours in all kinds of weather and toting their babies and children, led one to believe that their very lives depended on a visit. It saddens me to say I later learned that for some women, that latter statement rang true. Some women would drive from near and far, and stay overnight in nearby hotels, just to be the first one in line. Some women actually slept overnight in their cars with their babies. As a woman and a mother, I cannot comprehend their way of thinking.

Dreadfully, many of these women were arrested in the presence of their children before, during, and after a visit for attempting to smuggle in drugs, guns, knives, or any other type of contraband they could conceal on their person or inside their body cavities. Once the contraband was confiscated, she was handcuffed and detained until the local police arrived to make an official arrest. From there she would be transported to the county jail, where she would remain pending a bail hearing. In the meantime, the infant, child, or children would be released into the custody of the Child Protection Agency. Additionally, the women would be charged criminally, for endangering the welfare of a child. This was a common felony offense charged against the mothers and guardians of the children. It is the same felony offense for leaving the children unattended in their vehicles, in the bitter cold, or in sweltering heat from the time they stood outside in line until the visits ended. Keep in mind that this entire process could last for eight hours or more, especially when you consider the time frame from when they got in line until the visits ended.

Once the doors were finally opened, the registration process would start with a myriad of lies—beginning with the fake IDs. It was a draining process to say the least. If the visitors were not arrested or rejected for falsifying information, they then were required to go through the procedure of being frisked, scanned and sometimes, partially stripped searched. I am going to break this all down in the next chapter. These procedures were performed in advance of the prisoner being summonsed and escorted from his cell to the visit area. The prisoner had to conform to a completely nude body search prior to the initiation of his three-hour visit. On top of that, for obvious security reasons, all visitors were detained in the visit area until visits ended and all prisoners were cleared out of the area. Then the visitors were ushered out.

Visitors were not permitted to leave early or come and go as they pleased unless there was an emergency, or there was an inappropriate episode on the premises. Up until the corrections officers unlocked and unchained the steel doors and gates, everyone was a prisoner. All visitors are informed of this intransigent system before attempting to visit. Therefore, leaving their children in a car during the visit was a reprehensible act that reflected the desperation and disregard of both the male prisoner and his female visitor. I allude to a female visitor, rather than the mother in this instance, because there were plenty of times the women brought someone else's child to use the child to transport contraband. This relates back to the criminal offense of endangering the welfare of a child. It was more than evident that the prisoner and his female visitor were looking after their own interests and desires, without a care in the world other than committing crimes and having an intimate interaction. This was also indicative of the way that the children in the visit area were totally ignored during their visit. What has never ceased to amaze me is that, in such unsightly and deplorable surroundings, play areas were set aside for the children inside and outside of the visit area.

Whereas in the female prison, the one child had to remain seated at all times and holding visits outside, was unheard of. During visits at the male prison, if a child was seated, stagnant or not playing, they stood out like a sore thumb. Generally, this was a red flag. More than likely, the adults were doing something illicit and needed the child as a lookout or a body blocker. No, I didn't make a mistake in my writings; you read it correctly. The cold-hearted raw details are forthcoming in the following chapters, bear with me. Yes, the children were coerced into, or should I say, forced into becoming co-conspirators. The age of the child had no relevance.

In the same breath, I will tell you that the children who were freely playing in the designated areas were exceptionally unruly, mainly because their self-seeking guardians or parents were grossly ignoring them. Eventually, the children were running wild throughout the entire visit area, inside and outside. The supervision of the children, nine out of ten times, was monitored and controlled by the corrections officers. The unruliness, commotion and inappropriate sexual behavior made the visit area look more like a circus arena. It was an appalling sight to observe in the confines of a massive prison that housed some of the most hardened criminals alive, and where no one was safe.

In addition to this masquerade, I never gained clarity on the fact that there were special weekends for the prisoners and their families to have picnics. Weekend picnics in the abyss were nothing more than a charade. There was live musical entertainment performed by the prisoners, games for the children, and special food provided by the state for outdoor grilling. See if you can chew on that for a minute. I, for one, thought this was insane. As one of the many spectators on duty—because that's what the officers were reduced to—I became sickened every time I had to stand duty and watch this spectacle. The innocent children were doing what they do best, play and have fun lacking the full understanding of the reality of it all, they were locked in, walled in and fenced in by barbed wire inside of a massive institution doing what children do best: play and have fun.

It would break my heart knowing that the children really looked forward to those fun-filled weekend events. What child wouldn't? It made me wonder though. Eventually, when some of the children grew older, would they unconsciously look forward to going to prison, not differentiating or understanding, and so, believing that prison was a fun place to be? I do believe this is a state of mind known as unconscious irony. Forever mystified, I could not believe the lack of self-restraint, and what was openly happening in an extraordinarily unsafe environment among convicted felons, murderers, rapists, and above all else, pedophiles.

The ordeal of the visit program began to wear on my patience. It became deeply unsettling, as well as an arduous task. The male prisoners would dress to impress and patiently wait in their cells for an officer to escort them to the visit area, as if they were being led to a formal ball. It was rare that a male prisoner complained about rejection or disappointment. Unlike the female prisoner, the male prisoner had a list of women to choose from, and any one of them could show up for a visit. Their motto was "What one won't do, another one will." So often more than one female did show up. At that time, the prisoner was given the "privilege" to choose or have the pleasure of both women, depending on the litany of lies they conjured up. For instance, one would pretend to be his aunt, and the other may pretend to be his cousin.

On that same note, there were instances when one of the women was completely oblivious to the games, refused to play along, and left without a problem, never to come back. Others, were uncompromising triggering off a clash between the ill-fated rivals, by disputing over whom they felt "deserved" the visit. Yes, I said "deserved." Otherwise, they would concoct another story and share the visit, or simply, one would choose to come back on another visit day, which could very well be the next day. Now if the prisoner's "special" lady failed to show up for a visit, and he became angry enough, he had the option to remove her name from his list to make room for another naive female. Then again, that "special" lady may have to suffer the consequences for standing him up and embarrassing him in front of his boys. I have seen prisoners humiliate their female visitor just to show his control, or have a corrections officer cancel the visit, midstream, just because he had the prerogative. When this occurs, the prisoner is escorted back to his cell, and the female visitor has to remain in the visit center, humiliated, until visits were over. Many times the women would go through those long, drawn-out visit procedures to finally reach the visit center only to learn that the prisoner declined the visit and refused to come out of his cell—or that he had her name removed from his list without her knowledge. Then he would satisfy that void with another ingenuous female victim. No matter how you viewed it, it was a pathetic set of circumstances on all levels.

What made visit days even more offensive were the incidents in which a prisoner had to be accosted, handcuffed, and carted away to solitary confinement for physically assaulting his female visitor. The cockiness of their unexplainable explanations for their assaults varied from the female not showing up for a visit, to her arriving late, or simply, being disobedient as they'd put it in their audacious defense. As if any reason was justifiable. However, during the many investigations, the truth was discovered. The two major motives for the prisoner's violent behavior were (1) she refused to smuggle in contraband and (2) she refused to submit to a prohibited deviant sexual act right there on the spot during visits. Consequently, he would either beat her or threaten her into submission.

It was apparent that the same acts of violence that placed them behind bars were part of the ongoing list of crimes that continued to persist behind the wall. Let me shed light on, "beat her into submission." Prisoners have surreptitiously brought about bodily harm to their female visitors-turned-victims by sneaking in sudden blows to her body. Like quick sucker punches to her stomach, swift kicks to her legs, stepping or stomping on her feet, bending her fingers back, squeezing her hands, and severe pinching throughout her body, in some cases to the extent of drawing blood. This is miniscule and only some of the attacks that I personally witnessed.

Oh, I forgot about the biting. On one occasion, a prisoner acted like a wild beast when he sank his teeth into his girlfriend's arm, causing an injury savage enough to require stitches and a tetanus shot. Following his barbaric attack, an inadequate thirty-day ban on his visits was imposed. Soon thereafter, his visits were reinstated. When she returned—yes, she came back—it was clear that his bite mark would develop into a lifelong scar. She displayed it for all to see like a badge of honor. I was appalled at the naiveté of the females, young and old.

There are so many occurrences that stand out in my mind when I reflect on the brutal attacks on the women during a simple visit. There was one incident where we accosted a prisoner who was throwing a hissy fit concerning his girlfriend's outfit. According to him, her skirt was not short enough. While yelling to the top of his lungs all sorts of obscenities, he had the audacity to openly, and without reservation, slap her so hard in her face that the sound brought the noisy visit center to complete silence, capturing the attention of everyone, including the children. Once more a meager sanction was imposed, and they both received a time-out period like a form of punishment given to a child by a parent or a teacher.

Incidentally, the victims of any assault had every right to file charges but typically chose not to. However, since this assault had witnesses, the prisoner was charged with aggravated assault and sentenced to forty-five days in the hole. In the interim, like most of the female victims, his girlfriend waited with bated breath to receive a letter from him, informing her of the date his visits would be reinstated. And like a boomerang, she'd come right back. Too often, I felt as though my efforts to do my duty as a corrections officer were pointless.

There was another time, I came across the fiercest act of violence I have ever witnessed in my life. It was during visits when a prisoner began mercilessly choking his wife. The death grip he had around her neck was so strong and so tight that it took three male officers to loosen his grasp and several more officers to subdue him. By this time his wife was unconscious, when she helplessly fell to the concrete floor and cracked her skull. In his fit of rage, while being restrained, he persisted with his profane mouth as she lay lifeless. "You are lucky they pulled me off of you, bitch! I hope you die!" He was unquestionably on a fatal mission, brandishing his blatant disregard for life, and he was not going to stop until she was dead.

While all this was going on, the visit center was immobilized. The medics' futile attempts to revive her and sustain her life until the ambulance arrived were unsuccessful. She succumbed to his murderous attack before they arrived. After being in solitary confinement for a year, nonetheless, he merely exercised his rights and chose another potential fatality from the infamous visit list. Apparently, in spite of his heinous crime, his visits were reinstated. I guess I should make mention that he was on death row, signifying, he already was sentenced to life in prison for murder. He had nothing to lose. He was never going to be released from prison. The only way out for him was in a body bag. Imagine a convicted murderer, in prison, who commits another murder— of his visitor. Yet he was allowed to have more visits with more vulnerable potential victims. There was nothing to stop him from killing, and there seemed to be nothing to stop his visits. But after another attempt on someone else's life, his visits were only reduced to window visits. In the end, he ended up taking his own life because he didn't want to receive visits from the window.

From time to time, when a prisoner physically assaulted a visitor, it would go unnoticed because the visit center was so disruptive and crowded. The video surveillance camera picked up some of the assaults, along with some illegal transactions, but not nearly enough. The self-appointed confidential informants (CIs), better known as snitches, were scattered throughout the prison among the prisoners and officers. Consequently, that only hindered matters. A snitch on the inside is a form of trust on life support. This was one of the primary reasons why some women were so skeptical and shied away from alerting an officer regarding an assault or illegal activity.

It was as much of a catch-22 for me as it was for them. I would say even more so for me because of my position and my constant interaction with both men, prisoners and officers, on an array of issues other than visits. A few of the officers were blatant about their off-the-record ways; others chose to remain incognito. If you recall, that bone of contention relating to the trust factor with my colleagues began to dwindle when I was in the academy. From the very beginning of my career, it was evident that the trust factor was going to be a problem when it came to my colleagues, and of course, there was never a question when it came to the trust of a prisoner, or so I thought. I made this clear in the introduction when I said, "The only differences between these two men are the colors of their uniforms." However, having said that, at some point in the game you have to take your chances and trust somebody. It's a shame to say, but at times I received better results trusting a prisoner than trusting an officer.

In this game of survival, I tried to do my duty as diligently as possible, or as much as I was permitted to do so. For example, at the close of visits, I took the initiative to be exceptionally attentive. I purposely looked for fresh bruises on the exposed areas of the female visitor's body, such as her face, neck, arms and legs. I mainly looked for something that might point to a possible assault, something that was not present when she arrived. If, in fact, I did notice something, I would question them about it, hoping that they would want to file a charge. Those I approached refused to take advantage of the opportunity. Therefore, I stopped unless they approached me.

When visits were drawing to a close, everything seemed to go haywire and escalate into complete chaos. It was then, while saying their farewells, that the visitors would jump at the final chance to making feverish attempts, to pass off any contraband they were unable to hand over during the course of their visit, banking on the fact that they would not be noticed in the mass confusion. The rapid gyrating of their arms and hands made it virtually impossible to detect anything. In addition to the excessive hugging and touching, the long, drawn-out tongue kissing that was permitted was just an exaggerated way of trafficking. For these same reasons, the surveillance tapes were scrutinized in slow motion to capture any illegal transfers. The visit program for the men was the strategic enabler for infiltrating the prison with the bulk of drugs, weapons, and cash, besides the smuggling by corrections officers and employees.

During the male visits, the times were few and far between

when a female visitor was brave enough, or out of sheer fear, would alert me, or another officer about an unlawful transaction or assault. Whether it was verbally or through a subliminal gesture, the women were petrified, and so was I. Mutually feeling her skepticism was ominous. Regardless, I tried my best to help, as I mentioned earlier. For example, if a female visitor slipped up and notified an officer who, unbeknown to her, was a snitch, that officer would set her mind at ease. The officer would assure her that the proper protocol would be followed and the proper charges filed against the prisoner. In fact, this officer would do nothing and instead inform the prisoner of the allegations against him. This would leave the female in a vulnerable position because she believed the situation had been rectified. The scenarios were infinite. There were snitch officers who would expose a female visitor's and an officer's anonymity, especially if there was an officer who was legitimately doing their duty. This would put them both in a volatile position.

If everything went as it was supposed to in these scandalous plots, in due course the prisoner would be charged and subjected to additional jail time, and the visitor would be indefinitely barred from the institution. One of the worst-case scenarios, after going through one of these risky situations, is when female visitors backpedal, deny their involvement altogether, and then turn around and make a plea to the superintendent to have her visits reinstated, even after lying. This contributes to the revolving door that's created within the penal system.

Looking at the best-case scenario, it was a way out for some females because they were too afraid to confront the prisoner and let him know that she did not want to be involved in any criminal activity. Therefore, she would take a chance and alert an officer, hoping he or she was not a snitch. Other females would continue to visit out of absolute fear of retaliation if they did not visit or obey what the prisoner pressured them to do. Unbelievably, there were female visitors bullied into silence and fear by a corrupt officer, who was working either for the prisoner or on his own behalf for their deceitful reasons. I have seen prisoners threaten their own mothers for arriving late to a visit or for not obeying his orders. This type of arrogant behavior was preposterous. It has led me to believe that the prisoners presumed that their overwhelming sense of entitlement was warranted due to the almost unlimited privileges they were granted. With no financial obligations, they were eating and residing for free, and they were granted visits—rain or shine, inside or outside—three to four times a week, including window visits. Let us not forget about the special weekends set aside for live entertainment. Like spoiled brats, they were constantly given privileges in spite of their wrongdoing.

I stress these facts because I am convinced that the male prisoners developed this strong sense of entitlement, in part, because of the method in which the entire visit program was structured. I alluded to this earlier, but allow me to illustrate even further. The outside visit area was designed to look much like a park with benches, picnic tables, and canopies. The canopies were supposed to block the sun; instead they blocked their sexual their indiscretions and vicious assaults. Let me reiterate, conjugal visits were illegal. Despite this rule, females came to the visit center, lugging their newborns and small children who were conceived in this same prison. Moreover, what is prevalent in both the male and the female prisons is the perpetual cycle of male officers impregnating female prisoners and male prisoners impregnating female officers. This culminates in generations of families that are not only conceived but also born behind bars.

In the abyss, the visit program's code of behavior for the male prisoner and his female visitor was worthless. The prison officials made little effort to control the immoral sexual conduct and salacious behavior that went on in the presence of everyone in the visit center. At the female correctional facility, however, the code of behavior for the female prisoner and her visitor was strictly enforced. Listen, I have only scratched the surface of the male prison visits to give you some insight on the untold differences between their visit programs.

I can't say this enough: those prisoners who were committing the shameless acts of overt sex and violent assaults had no regard for the other visitors, including the children and the elderly. They should have been banned from visits for their lewdness and lack of respect. It was only once in a blue moon that a visitor was permanently banned. And if so, it just gave the prisoner the opportunity to choose another visitor.

Supposedly, the visit program was intended to suppress the prisoner's propensity to cause further infringements while behind bars and allow them to release some tension from being locked away from society. However, the joy of actually having the privilege to have a tangible visit with their loved ones went from a source of happiness to a source of corruption. By committing more crimes, the prisoners defeated the purpose of visits. In addition to the obvious, it also allowed more criminals to enter the abyss.

Please do not get the wrong impression from my narratives. There were scores of women with self-respect and integrity who visited their loved ones. On the same token, there were scores of male prisoners who respected and appreciated their visits from loved ones. Tragically, the women who had good intentions were sometimes strong-armed into committing crimes, or they became victims of sexual and physical abuse right under the watchful eye of the prison officials.

On the contrary, there were those females and males who brought their criminal state of mind to the visit center, magnifying the distortion and corruption from within. These were the ones who had no respect for themselves or anyone else—most of all, their own children. Too many of the females had a subservient personality and were ready and willing to do anything and everything the prisoner asked them to do—even at the expense of their children and their children's innocence; and even at the cost of their freedom. Ultimately, sometimes at the cost of their own precious lives. Now I will leave nothing to the imagination about the male prisoner's visit program.

SEARCH, SEX, AND SEIZURE: THE MALE PRISONER'S VISIT PROGRAM

UPON ENTERING THE ABYSS FOR a visit, everyone was regarded as a potential visitor. If a person violated one of the rules or dress codes during the initial search process, their anticipated visit was denied. Everyone was subjected to a screening by a hand-held metal detector operated by a corrections officer. This procedure was performed before walking through a scan machine, with their shoes and socks removed and placed on a conveyor belt, followed by a physical pat down, better known as a pat frisk. The procedures are equivalent to the screenings at the major airports. In this prison, though, the male officers patted down the men, and the female officers patted down the women and children. Therefore, my hands were full since the male prison's visit program was swarming with women and children.

If the scan machine detected something on the visitor's person or just didn't work properly, which was most of the time, a more thorough search was conducted with additional officers and a sergeant present. At that point, the potential visitor had to conform to a more detailed search of their person and the items they were authorized to bring into the prison, which was not that much. Unless, they were bringing babies and young children. Only then, were they permitted to bring in items that were a necessity like baby bottles, baby bags, and disposable diapers. These items had to be searched along with their pockets, shoes, socks, and whatever else the officers deemed suspicious. Additional items, such as handbags, backpacks and wallets were not allowed inside the prison. These personal belongings had to be left in their vehicles or in a locker provided by the DOC.

Every child from a newborn to the age of seventeen, was subjected to this thorough search with the verbal and signed consent of the parent or guardian. If the adult did not consent to the search of the minor child or refused because of the search procedures, their visit was denied. In rare cases, their visits were banned, due to suspicion of illegal activity. In fact, every adult bringing children was meticulously searched with the children in a private room. The sad fact behind this stipulation, was that there were way too many mothers and guardians using the children as tools to smuggle in contraband.

Just to recap, it was a well-known fact that the female visitor, with or without children, was one of the main sources of contraband, besides the corrections officers. Unfortunately, the upright female visitors who were there for a simple visit, were highly frustrated by this search practice, and rightfully so.

Not every female who visited with children was using them as smugglers.

Our focus was not only directed at women with children, but it was a primary concern. Certainly, the male visitors, and even the elderly, were involved in these trafficking schemes. I recall an incident in which an elderly woman had traveled from out of state to visit her son. Before I could say or do anything, she informed me that she had a prosthetic leg, and she did not want to walk through the scan machine. That being the case, she automatically exposed herself to an even more meticulous search, which involved her prosthetic leg. This search was considered a visitor's strip search, which is quite different from the prisoner's strip search. A prisoner must strip down to his or her birthday suit; whereas, a visitor only has to remove certain articles of their clothing, such as a sweater, a jacket, shoes, and socks. Then they are systematically patted down. For some reason, this elderly woman was under the impression that because of her disability, she was excluded from all searches, which instantly made me leery. Her son was incarcerated too long for her not to know.

She became seriously upset when I tried to break down the protocol, telling her that not only did she have to submit to a visitor's strip search in a private room, but she also had to remove her prosthetic leg in the process. It had to be inspected as well. She became outraged and demanded to speak with the warden. She insisted on making a complaint against me for discrimination. Her tirade went on for about fifteen minutes.

In the interim, a female lieutenant and I were being as polite as possible, trying to explain to her that she was losing precious time to visit with her son. We informed her that her son would not be called out of his cell until she was searched and cleared for the visit. We called ourselves looking out for her best interest, by trying to avoid summonsing the warden over the radio. We were making every effort to prevent her from being totally humiliated. It wasn't like she didn't know that I had spoken with him over the phone on her behalf.

When the warden finally came strolling in, almost thirty minutes or so into this fiasco, he reiterated precisely what I had tried my best to do in vain. I knew his involvement would fan the flames and increase the woman's stress level when he harshly informed her, "Either you submit to the search, or I will have you thrown out of here!" Then he abruptly exited the room, without listening to a word she had to say. She became so infuriated that she started to hyperventilate, wasting more time. We simply echoed the warden and reminded her that she had a few minutes to calm down and comply because she was on the verge of losing out on a visit with her son, which would be heartbreaking after traveling from such a long distance. The whole procedure was uncomfortable and embarrassing for us all, but it was something that had to be done.

After nearly an hour, she finally complied, and her visit with her son was cut in half, all due to her defiance. Her performance, however, ended up becoming a regular routine. Each time she visited, she made a scene. After some time, her actions were considered suspicious due to their repetitive nature. They were distracting, but we didn't know if they were intentional diversions for some kind of illegal activity. Inevitably, she was banned from the institution.

This prison also housed a K-9 unit of professionally trained dogs with a keen sense of smell. Once visits convened, the vehicles in the visitor parking lot were randomly searched by the K-9 unit. If a vehicle came under suspicion, it was seized and searched. Additionally, this special task force was the source for discovering children and pets locked inside of the vehicles during the visits. Subsequently, the owners of the vehicles were arrested upon exiting visits. Anytime a visitor was arrested before, during or after a visit, the affiliated prisoner was questioned and held in solitary confinement pending an investigation. Even with the massive scale of strict guidelines, searches and seizures, the prison was infested with contraband from the streets. The prisoners and the like-minded criminals who flooded the gates for a visit were exceptionally resourceful.

As a female corrections officer, I was under intense pressure on many levels regarding the female visitors. Besides the smuggling issues, we had to focus on their attire since there was a strict dress code in place. Even before the registration process commenced, the officers were required to inspect the long lines of visitors outside to ascertain that the women were appropriately dressed. If a woman was inappropriately or provocatively dressed, sometimes it was an indication that she was prepared to engage in sexual misconduct.

The females also dressed seductively because they wanted to put on a show for the men—the officers and the prisoners. It was sickening, but they yearned to be in the running for a chance to have their names affixed to a prisoner's visit list and become a woman of ill repute. They dressed like raunchy prostitutes who walked the streets in search of a john, or pimp. In this case, their prospective john was a prisoner, or possibly an officer, who would have his eyes fixated on her like a dog in heat. From there, she would be used for everything from sex trafficking to drug trafficking. I mentioned male officers because she could achieve favors through them by using sex as a bartering tool. Leaving nothing to the imagination when it came to her attire didn't always mean sex; she could be appropriately dressed, and they would still achieve illicit sex.

In any case, if I could determine from a visual that a female visitor was inappropriately dressed, I, along with some other officers, would give her the opportunity to go back to her car and retrieve something more suitable to wear, or go to the nearby strip mall and purchase something more appropriate. Yes, the strip mall. This pinpoints how long they waited in line and how desperate they were for a visit. Swapping certain articles of clothing to adhere to the dress codes was common practice among the women standing outside in line, even though they were, in some cases, complete strangers to one another. Exchanging sweaters, blouses, or T-shirts to cover up their exposed cleavages, belly buttons, or the cracks of their backside was nothing for them, just as long as they got inside to visit.

These last-minute modifications depended on the officers and whether or not they would give them the courtesy to make these swaps, quick runs, or changes. Technically, her visit was supposed to be declined once it was determined that she was dressed inappropriately. They would literally beg the officers to do whatever was necessary, including having sex, to avoid being rejected from visiting. At times I found myself afraid for the women or feeling sorry for some of them, no matter what they did. Some women were so nervous, believing that if they were declined a visit due to a mistake on her part, there would be guaranteed repercussions, whether it was inside the visit center or outside on the streets.

Occasionally, the women were so underdressed that it was impossible for her to adjust her clothing. Other times, it was too late to make that quick run to the strip mall. In those cases, I had no other alternative but to deny her a visit. But don't forget how often the male prisoners were allowed to receive visits. So, some females readily complied upon being rejected, knowing they could come right back the next day. Every now and then, a defiant female challenged my authority and forced me to write a report that resulted in her future visits being indefinitely cancelled. Of course, this did not stop the prisoner from receiving other female visitors. The male officers and prisoners had no shame during their outspoken disrespectful discussions about the women, female officers included. The female attention-seekers would surely be the topic of discussions in the visit center, turning heads as they constantly pranced back and forth, from their seats to the vending machines, the restroom, and anywhere else that prompted them to leave their seats, as long as they could be seen.

No one could keep up with how many times she would intentionally drop something, so that she could bend over and pick it up for those who wanted to get a quick sneak peek. These gullible females would end up being passed from one prisoner's visit list to another's, and from one officer to another. Meanwhile, she becomes more and more subservient until the men grew tired of her. Then, she is deemed useless, her name is removed from the list, and she is dismissed. Useless in one prison, she travels to another prison, and the disgraceful process repeats itself. Soon thereafter, the never-ending cycle of new fresh meat is brought into the visit center.

It was a harsh reality, dealing with females, young and old, and witnessing the extreme lengths they went to for attention and the outright disrespect they endured. I remember vividly the nervousness in many of their beautiful eyes as they walked in with such innocent glee and then walked out heartbroken, ashamed, and terrified, vowing never to return. Yet, defying themselves, they would return weary and teary eyed, lost and confused. More to the point, though, these women were trained to be the principal suppliers and smugglers of the prison. While much of our focus was on the female visitors and the children, the corrections officers also had to pay close attention to the male visitors. There was a dress code in place for them too, but the protocol was slightly different. By this I mean the men were prohibited from wearing hats, jackets, and coats inside the visit center. In truth, this protocol was the same for all visitors. The only difference was that the officers were required to keep a close eye on the male visitor's footwear when entering and exiting, to make sure he was wearing exactly the same footwear when leaving.

The reason behind these specifics was that an officer once noticed a ten-year-old boy wearing an oversized pair of boots, large enough to fit a man. The young boy could barely keep them on his feet as he stumbled into the visit center. The child's mother, in her ignorance, explained to the officer that her boyfriend, the prisoner, told her that making the swap would not be a problem. She forgot to forget, that it was supposed to be a secret. It was at that point we realized the male visitors were exchanging footwear with the prisoners. Thus, the male officers who did the strip searches of the prisoners before and after visits were obligated to take a detailed account of the type of footwear the prisoners were wearing. Every so often, even some of the female visitors were caught wearing men's footwear in an attempt to make a swap during visits.

Clearly, these exchanges were another conspired smuggling scheme and difficult to maintain. Additionally, when street clothing was delivered by mail, it was thoroughly examined, and naturally, a heap of contraband was seized. Eventually, the prisoners were banned from wearing shoes and clothing from the outside.

In my strip searches of the prisoners and visitors, I confiscated the strangest things in the strangest places, and I am sure that every officer has a ton of weird stories to tell. This leads me to the overall standard systematic searches, where we primarily focused on the seizing of contraband. Aside from the fact that our primary concern was confiscating contraband from the visitors, as a female officer, my searches led me far beyond a regular search and seizure.

One key concern was preventing the repulsive sexual behavior that the prison officials had the reluctance or the inability to control. Therefore, while in the process of searching for the contraband that was flooding the gates of the prison, the female officers also were required to ascertain whether the female visitors were wearing underwear—yet another demeaning task. Without overstating this embarrassing assessment, it was as close to a physical examination as you could get, without having them disrobe. To circumvent this awkward process, I would come straight out and ask, "Are you wearing a bra and panties?"

Since the absence of one or both was a mandated rejection of her visit, that would rid me of the dreaded, drawn-out procedure of the pat frisk. However, it was not always that easy because there were those who thought they could get away with anything. Some would outright lie about the most obvious things, and during the search, I would find out that she was not wearing any underwear, when she professed that she was. What she was required to do was to pull up the seam of her panties, making it visible for the officer to see if she was wearing pants or a skirt. If she was wearing a dress, she had to snap back the seam of her panties through the dress, but that could very well be a G-string, which was prohibited. The same concept applied for their bras, especially because the bra was a major concealer of contraband. I would suggest that they unfasten their bra strap and shake it, rather than feel around on her breast area, which we were supposed to do. There were so many instances in which they would have the contraband taped to their breast or their bra. But it didn't matter how thorough the officers were with their pat frisks and searches; the visitors found ways to get around them. They wore other prohibited articles of lingerie, such as thongs and snap-away, edible, and crotchless panties.

Every so often, they would get cold feet and just come right out and confess. Some were smart enough to sidestep the silliness of it all, and as soon as she was cleared to go inside, she would simply go into the bathroom and remove her underwear, period. In addition, they wore pants with makeshift cut-out holes, rips and tears in the crotch area. This created an avenue for easy access for the prisoner to penetrate his penis, his fingers, his hands, or any other object into her vagina or rectum, for his sexual gratification, or to retrieve implanted contraband. The creativity and ingenuity they possessed to engage in all sorts of unlawful and unspeakable acts proved they had no inhibitions whatsoever.

Their unrelenting indiscretions are a huge part of prison life. Therefore, it never stopped being a challenge for me as an officer, a female, a mother, and a morally conscious human being. I was determined not to become institutionalized like the prisoners, the visitors, and too many of my peers. I fought daily against becoming immune to the outlandish behavior that will never cease inside the prisons. The rules and regulations of the DOC are exceedingly and morally ambiguous, which gives rise to the already difficult duties of a corrections officer. The dress-code violations were relentlessly contested and disputed. Basically, women were not allowed to wear dresses, skirts, or shorts above the knee. They also were prohibited from wearing sleeveless, strapless, backless, and sheer blouses. It is impossible to go through the entire dress code, and it was virtually impossible to adhere to all of the restrictions, especially when you take into account that the prisoner's and visitor's resourcefulness was infinite. The DOC could not keep up with the never-ending illegal transactions and the exhausting attempts to implement new rules.

There is no such thing as a moral compass in prison. There

were times when a prisoner would physically try to fight off the corrections officer if he and his female culprit were caught having sex. It was much like two dogs stuck together during sexual intercourse; if a person attempted to pull the dogs apart, the male dog usually turns around and tries to bite that person. That is exactly the way these episodes played out. Nothing stopped them from engaging in sex, while in the interim, making babies. What's even more alarming is that they had no qualms about using their own children, or someone else's child, as a lookout, while engaging in the vilest ways. I cannot stress enough how innocent children were helplessly bred to be future criminals. When a mother forces her child to be a lookout for her while she voluntarily or involuntarily performs oral sex, that, in and of itself, is a crime and a serious form of child neglect that constitutes child endangerment.

Before I go any further, I was discussing the strip-search process before I veered into their salacious sexual behavior in the prisons. I will get back into sexual improprieties a little further on in this segment. Meanwhile, let me continue with the search process for female visitors that occurs before the sex and seizure. The female visitors' intricate searches were conducted from their hair and the inside of their wigs to the bottom of their feet and down to the soles of their shoes. The search began by examining wigs, toupees (male visitors), hairpieces, scarves, and headpieces, such as religious headdresses, that had to be removed, and thoroughly examined. In doing these searches, I have found the most unexpected things. I have confiscated prescriptions, over-the-counter drugs, and street drugs, such as heroin, cocaine, and crack, along with hypodermic needles. These were just some of the things that were attached, stapled, pinned, glued, or somehow wedged into their hair, wigs, and headdresses. And these were some of the same items, as well as other contraband, that were lodged inside of their body cavities, ears, noses, and mouths.

The infirmary, which is the medical wing in the prison, or a local hospital would retrieve the deep-rooted objects from within their vaginas and rectums—that's if the prisoner did not get there first. Additionally, contraband could be taped anywhere on any part of their outer body like the leg, arm, back, stomach, etc. Moreover, I have seized deadly narcotic prescriptions and over-the-counter drugs, liquid medications, and all types of pills planted in the tiny pockets of infants' and children's clothing. This would make my head spin, knowing that at any given moment, one of these lethal drugs could have been easily swallowed due to their innocence. The children were simply used as pawns. As I've said repeatedly, that was the visitors' only purpose for bringing the children in the first place.

During these unpleasant searches, we have detected the smell of liquor and discovered vodka and rum in an infant's bottle, giving the appearance of water and apple juice. As a result, water and juice were prohibited from being brought into the prison. These items had to be purchased inside from the vending machines. (I didn't elaborate on the vending machines located in the visit area, exclusively for the visitors' and prisoners' dining pleasure.) Nevertheless, this new rule drove the culprits to stoop to an all-time low. They went so far as to pour the liquor into the infant's milk, because they could no longer substitute the liquor for the infant's water or juice.

If you can stomach what I have just told you, perhaps your comprehension can withstand these facts. By contaminating the baby's source of food by pouring liquor into their milk bottles, the mothers or guardians, also allow their babies to cry in hunger for the duration of the visit because they would run out of the baby's milk supply as it was devoured by the prisoner who was now intoxicated. Just imagine being trapped inside of a massive institution with intoxicated, drug-induced serial rapists, murderers, and incorrigible psychopaths. This is an everyday occurrence behind the walls of the prisons.

To somewhat rectify the identifiable violations, the DOC limited the amount of milk bottles allowed inside to suppress the consumption of alcohol. This, however, ended up becoming a double-edged sword because the babies were hungry and the prisoners were drunk. Thus, the corrections officers were ordered to open every single milk bottle and sniff for the presence of hard-core liquor. It blows my mind to think that all of these criminally suggestive behaviors, primarily by females, were attempted and/or accomplished merely to satisfy the prisoner at whatever sacrifice.

During my twenty-five-year tenure, I could not help but notice that the elder mothers were supplying their incarcerated sons with contraband and young girls for the prisoners' deviant sexual pleasures—similar to the younger mothers, who were using their small children as smugglers and lookouts on visit days. Seemingly, they were teaching their children how to become criminals, preparing them for a life of imprisonment. I found this to be the most heartless form of predictable patterns of crimes that I could imagine.

Now back to the searches. I have confiscated cassette tapes, cash, drugs and weapons, such as folding knives, box cutters and nail files. Sometimes they were placed in plastic baggies that were protruding from a female's vagina or rectum. Many times during a search, the female would pull the item out because it was causing her excruciating pain. The discovery of the cassette tape stands out in my memory. It was protruding from a female's vagina, and just by chance, I heard a rattling sound as I was performing the pat frisk. Curious, I patted her up and down once again, and my hand bumped the plastic case. After grilling her for about twenty seconds, she told me what it was and gently pulled it out. The new cassette tape, still in its unopened plastic case, was dripping with blood. Then she pleaded with me not to confiscate it and suggested that I throw it away. At that point in the game, I thought nothing could surprise me. I merely shook my head in disgust. Needless to say, I had to place her in handcuffs and detain her until the local police arrived.

Reprehensibly, the children were never excluded from any of these barbaric criminal acts, not even from having the contraband inserted into their tiny, precious body cavities. I know, it goes far beyond words. The female visitors also used tampons and sanitary napkins as smuggling tools until these items were prohibited from being brought inside. If a female visitor was menstruating, she had to inform a female officer, who provided her with as many feminine products as she needed, all at the expense of the DOC. Since they were unable to use their own personal disposables, the women resorted to their baby's disposable diapers. The officers would find soiled, bloody diapers in the female's bathroom. I don't know why either, if that's what you're wondering. Perhaps they felt a bit of shame or fear and didn't want to ask a corrections officer for assistance. Quite often the prisoners warned their female visitors to stay away from us.

In addition to these dreadful searches, visitors were required to open their mouth and lift up their tongue, somewhat in accordance with the prisoners' search protocol. On one occasion, I observed a regular female visitor who appeared to be unusually nervous as she was being searched. This was not the norm for her. When I asked her to open her mouth and lift up her tongue, my suspicions were confirmed. Never in my wildest dreams would I have imagined what she was concealing under her tongue. It was a key to a pair of handcuffs. She quickly removed it from her mouth and surrendered without a problem, as if she could not wait to take it out of her mouth. Then she readily complied with the procedures and placed it into the evidence bag. I was convinced that she was relieved to get rid of it before it eased its way into the abyss of the prison.

Where and how did she retrieve a handcuff key that was the property of the DOC? That was anyone's guess. This pertinent information was never brought to light during the internal investigation and was something she never divulged. She was immediately arrested for unlawful possession of a state prison's handcuff key. She was convicted and sentenced to several years to a women's maximum security prison for aiding and abetting a state prisoner. The prisoner was her brother, who received additional time and was remanded to another institution, where he remained in the Enforced Isolation Unit (EIU) serving an additional five years consecutive to his prior lengthy sentence.

The EIU unit is a section of the prison equivalent to solitary confinement. The difference is that there are hundreds of prisoners housed in this unit as opposed to solitary confinement, where there are about seventy-five to one hundred prisoners. The EIU is also where prisoners are remanded upon sentencing after being temporarily held in the hole, pending an investigation. It's another jail within the jail. Let me enlighten you a bit about the EIU. It's much larger and located apart from the prison, but on the same property. For one hour once a day, the prisoner is released outside into a very small yard with two or three other prisoners, four being the max. This is similar to solitary confinement procedures.

Before going outside for one hour they are guarded by two armed officers to begin the process of taking a shower. Before exiting his cell, the prisoner is instructed to remove every stitch of his clothing, place his back against the cell door, and push his hands through the cubbyhole, a small opening in the steel door of a cell. This allows the officers to handcuff him from behind before they unlock the cell door. From there, he is ushered, completely naked, to the shower, which is also a cellblock. Then the same procedure is done in reverse. He steps inside the shower cell, the door is locked, and he places his back against the cell door, pushing out his handcuffed wrists through the cubbyhole so the officers can remove the handcuffs. Then he is permitted to have a three-minute shower. Without delay, the shower water is shut off, and those same procedures are repeated. He's led out of the shower, handcuffed and naked, directly back to his cell where he remains until he's permitted out again for that one hour.

Now, let me resume with the search and seizure. There was another time during a regular pat frisk that I recovered a single bullet from the skirt pocket of an elderly woman, who had been visiting her son for over fifteen years. The bullet belonged to a rifle (M-16) that just so happened to be the same type of rifles we carried. Again, this goes far beyond words. She asserted that she was completely oblivious as to how a bullet got into her pocket, claiming that it did not belong to her and she had never seen it before. Almost instantly, she began to cry when I made it clear that she was facing some serious criminal charges. Taking her age and frail posture into consideration, I tried to get her to leave the line, on her own accord, so we could proceed in private.

She knew that she was about to be arrested because out of nowhere, she went into a frenzy from sobbing tears to boiling with anger. She was unwilling to leave the area. To my dismay, I had no choice but to forcibly put her into restraints right there on the spot. It was hurtful for me to place handcuffs over her frail wrists. This simply points to my earlier theory about the unstable relationships between mothers and their incarcerated sons. Not surprisingly, she ended up serving time in prison, and her son was transferred to another prison, where he was sentenced to serve additional time. She was one of the many mothers who came to visit with criminal intent and left in handcuffs. It's extremely troubling to know that there were plenty of others who came with the same intent, some toting their children, believing they could get away with a crime by using the innocent little ones as scapegoats. They, too, left the visit center in handcuffs, and their children were taken away by protective child services.

The criminal activities that I have discussed in this section are mainly about the searching and seizing of contraband during the male visit program. The other concern during the male visits was the overt sexual behavior that I briefly touched on, which is a major interference and distraction in the prisons. The fact is the visits overall turned into a circus arena, and a major portion of the visits resembled a brothel— "a house of ill repute," as my grandmother would say. The prisoners and their female visitors, or male visitors, would achieve sexual intercourse in ways that were unconscionable, directly in front of the other visitors. Some of them thought they were being discreet, and others were just downright thoughtless in their actions.

I've repeated this over and over: there is no moral compass in the prison. Their overt sexual behavior was utterly disgraceful, more like sexual objectification. I use that term because the prisoners treated females as sexual objects with no consideration for her feelings, dignity, or respect. I can go as far as saying it was sadistic since some of the prisoners achieved sexual gratification by any means necessary. For example, they used physical force during sex by inflicting pain and causing injury to the female and, on occasion, to their male lovers. The unfortunate visitors, from grandparents to children and other relatives, who were there to have a pleasant visit with their loved ones, were totally disregarded and disgusted by the prisoners' complete lack of shame. My reaction also was invariably one of disgust when or if I had to intervene and seize their perverted actions.

I am going to try to characterize the sexual improprieties that dominated the male visit center. I will do my best to be as candid as possible without being distasteful. Previously, I explained that the outside visit area was designed like a park with benches and picnic tables. This same area was surrounded by colossal concrete walls and sealed throughout with barbed wire. This was where much of the lewd, deviant sex took place because it was a little more spacious with shaded areas—hot spots, as they were called. The "privileged" prisoners conveniently chose these areas to engage in sex, although it was illegal. The sex in these areas was deliberately uncontrolled. This is not to say that their sexual shenanigans were not as audacious inside the visit center.

At the time of these appalling episodes, every so often the officers were given permission to intervene. On other occasions, higher-ranking officers gave specific orders to "let them be," literally leaving the door open for the prisoners to do as they pleased. More than likely, these officers were in cahoots with the prisoners who were committing these sexual transgressions. Surely, that left the door wide open for other illegal dealings, namely drug trafficking. The male officers were straightforward when making it known: "It's a man's thing." That sentiment resonated throughout the prison. It was definitely a personal thing among the men. On too many occasions, it was explained to me that "a man has to bust that nut and relieve himself. This is how we keep the prison calm." What's more, it was understood that these were some of the self-proclaimed snitches and drug suppliers in the prison, who were doing all of this talking. I'm referring to the officers.

As I have indicated, besides giving them the opportunity to engage in sex, it was apparent that contraband was being exchanged at the same time because some of these prisoners didn't have to undergo the legal mandatory strip searches. Accordingly,

I was impelled to mind my own business unless I was directly pulled into one of the situations. The last thing I wanted to do was reveal to a prisoner or an officer that there was a conflict between us, especially concerning their illegal dealings between one another. Usually, both criminals knew whom to approach when it came to their unscrupulous dealings. The male bond was dogmatic and passionate. They tried to create an atmosphere where females were only to be seen and not heard—unless you were a female who was easily manipulated, be it officer, visitor, attorney, nurse, doctor, clergy, or any other female employee.

As far as I was concerned, it was crucial to stay away from the riffraff and stand my ground. Fortunately for me, that was my way of living while growing up. The perpetrators kept their distance, and I kept mine. Anyway, there were plenty of loose ends, meaning corrupt officers, for their devious minds to choose from. With all that being said, the sex could start from any place or position. Shockingly enough, the females were allowed to sit on the prisoner's lap. Sometimes they would stand very close together, and he would firmly hug her from behind for long periods of time. Keep in mind, the makeshift rips, cuts, and tears for easy access. You can only imagine what was happening.

Allowing a female visitor to sit on a prisoner's lap or stand very close together, in my opinion, were unreasonably liberal to begin with. Remember the rules set in place for the female prisoners during their visits? One could not even look hard at a female prisoner without being escorted out of the institution. Well, in the male prison, couples could fondle one another all day long. Sitting or standing, they made it appear as though nothing was going on but a little affection. However, if you looked long enough, it was plain to see that the prisoner was penetrating her with his hand or his penis. Again, either she did not have on any panties, or they made the penetration possible through the self-made holes. This is what they considered inconspicuous.

Some of their other methods were outrageously overt. For instance, one couple was so heavily engaged in sex that in the heat of the moment, the prisoner had the nerve to take a defensive stance. He went so far as to resist arrest by attacking the officers who were trying to intervene. There were similar incidents when officers, after a struggle with the prisoner, were finally able to pull him out of the female's vagina or rectum, exposing his erect penis, dripping with semen, as he fought like a wild dog with the officers. In the meantime, his female culprit found herself standing alone and dumbfounded. In the interim, I would be mortified along with the rest of the visitors—and let us not forget about the children.

From that point, it was my duty as one of the female officers to take an incident report from the female visitor, informing her of her right to file rape charges. Then I would escort her to the women's bathroom so she could compose herself and perhaps explain her actions. As mentioned, it was rare that they followed through by filing a charge of sexual aggravated assault, which constitutes rape. Let me put it like this: throughout my career, not one female ever filed any charges. Consequently, she and the prisoner would receive a cooling-off period. I will say it again: they both would receive a cooling-off period, believe it or not, until the next visit day. Moreover, that solely depended on the prisoner's status within the institution, relating back to the so-called privileged prisoner.

Some prisoners were bold enough to take a visitor, female or male, into a blind spot, whether they went willingly or unwillingly, and coerce them to bend over. Then the prisoner penetrated them from behind, performing anal sex and at times knocking the visitor's head against the wall. In some cases, the prisoner would gag them to stifle the sounds of their pain or pleasure. It was as if they were filming a hard-core porno flick in the privacy of a staged studio. When carrying out these acts of vulgarity, they had no shame in asking other prisoners, visitors, and their minor children to be lookouts or to block them from an officer's view. In other instances, the prisoner would fondle the female's breasts in plain view, even while a baby was sitting on her lap, using the child as a shield.

I know I have said this before, but sadly most times that was their only reason for bringing the children in the first place. And you thought that these situations involving children could not possibly get any worse. Well, think again. The conditions inside the prisons are hopeless. It is particularly difficult for the prisoners who are struggling to rehabilitate themselves. The insidious crimes involving children are indefinable. The prisoner's fondling went even deeper, figuratively and literally speaking. He would sometimes put his hand inside the female's crotch area and fondle her between her legs, up her dress, inside her pants, and either from the front or from the back, all while the child was sitting on her lap and watching and undergoing, the motions of the prisoner's hand movements. To add to this tragedy, the child had better not budge, or he or she would be admonished or spanked. The female would reciprocate by putting her hands inside the prisoner's groin area and fondle his genitals as well—or, even worse, use her mouth to perform fellatio. Once again, this all occurred in the presence of the bewildered children. The child's age had no bearing on the matters at hand, so long as they were breathing and could follow the adults' demands.

By now, I am sure you get the despicable picture of their sexually offensive and degrading behavior. I would be underplaying myself if I said that visit days were not an emotionally draining experience. It was hard to believe, but they came with something new and different every single time. Their ingenuity is limitless. It was not only unsettling to witness, but it is just as unsettling to put into words. Particularly when you think of the innocent children who were dragged into their tangled web of indecency, deception, and immorality.

Let me say this about prison love affairs, which are an integral part of what goes on behind the wall. A large number of the women who visited at the beginning of these prison relationships were sincere and wanted to believe that their love interactions defined the quintessential relationship. This is why, other than fear and lack of self-respect, they were willing to go out on a limb to please their incarcerated lovers. I have spoken with many female visitors over the years, and their rationale behind this belief, for the most part, was that they thought it was impossible for the prisoner to be unfaithful with another woman because he was locked away from society. This assumption, along with what I have discussed in the preceding chapters, has brought me to the following statement of facts. More than likely, if he was a womanizer on the outside, he was going to find a way to be one on the inside. It is too easy with the DOC at the helm. Little did the women know, or just didn't want to accept, was the fact that he was having sex on a regular basis with other male prisoners and male officers on the down low (DL). Or he was having sex with other female visitors and female officers and anyone else on the personnel staff who was willing or easily manipulated.

As time went on, the women eventually found out about their infidelities, but they were too submerged in superficial love, ignorance, or illegal ties to let go. They allowed their logic to be overruled by their emotions. These loyal and devoted—or should I say, naive and ignorant—females visited their incarcerated lovers religiously and performed various lewd and illicit sex acts, not to mention the drug trafficking and importing of other contraband at the risk of their own lives and freedom. There were women who stood by the prisoner's side for years, from the inception of his incarceration until his release. When that time came, however, she'd be the last person to learn that he had been freed from prison—only finding out when she came for her routine visit, and then informed by an officer, that he was no longer incarcerated and his whereabouts were confidential.

I have seen some women become so incredulous at that moment that they had to be physically ejected from the prison grounds and warned not to return or they would be arrested for trespassing. Still, some would return in utter disbelief or denial, hoping that he was still locked away from the outside world. Some women knew deep down in their hearts that there was a possibility of this fateful outcome, but they continued to visit despite the circumstances. Most had no idea of the prisoner's actual release date. Therefore, what they claimed to be a quintessential relationship was merely a figment of their imagination. This is yet another tragic set of circumstances that will always exist in prison love and life.

Getting back to the pat frisks, as a female corrections officer, I performed daily pat frisks on the male prisoners, but I was not required to conduct a completely nude strip search. There were definitely enough male officers for that unpleasant assignment. A female corrections officer only conducted a nude body search of a male prisoner during a crisis, such as a prison lockdown or an escape. I was especially appreciative for that at the closing of visits, after they had been engaged in their revolting sexual misconduct. It was sickening enough to see an occasional ejaculation of semen seeping through their pants or an unfulfilled erection after a failed attempt at sex. I saw enough of that during my night tour duties when I walked the plank/tier individually inspecting a prisoner's cellblock.

On one occasion I came upon a prisoner who was intentionally exposing his genitals and masturbating precisely at the time of head count, for lack of a better word. Everyone in the prison was well aware of the fact that the count, and the time frame associated with it, was of the utmost importance. That being the case, I could not disrupt the flow of counting for something so frivolous. The body count is the most pivotal time in all prisons. It occurs routinely every several hours throughout the day, and from time to time it's done randomly. During this time, every prisoner must be accounted for to determine that there are no escapes or dead corpses lying around. This is the only time that the entire institution is at a complete standstill, other than a lockdown, until the warden's office establishes that all the numbers are accurate and announces that the count is clear.

While the institution was at its standstill and the prisoners were locked in their cells, I took advantage of that opportunity to go back and confront the perverted prisoner who was exposing himself. My intention was to embarrass him by sensationalizing his actions. Once I got to his cell I spoke as loudly as possible, verbally emasculating him while his cellmates tuned in. I knew my little exhibition would cause him to stop the nonsense, at least in my presence. I made sure the prisoners were all tuned in because, as a whole, they considered masturbation problematic for their tier, especially when it was done in front of a female officer who found it disrespectful—not all females felt that way. But for those who did, like myself, and was the assigned officer on duty, that little episode could create a problem for the entire tier.

What I am saying is one bad apple can destroy the whole tree, meaning one messes up and they all suffer. Therefore, I knew they were going to admonish him. His perverted ways could very well cause problems for them all later on down the road when they were out on the tier performing their duties and needed more time or some other small favor. For example, it could be something as simple as wanting to speak to another prisoner or asking to stay in the shower or on the phone for one minute longer. Every little thing mattered. Without fail, a corrections officer has to be conscious of the fact that prison living is psychological warfare. Masturbation was also used as an intimidation tactic for new female recruits and other female employees who really felt grossed out about it. Masturbating in the presence of another was also a violation of the disciplinary rules, despite that the prisoners still did it every so often in front of anyone they felt would be intimidated or aroused. To be clear, some folks liked it.

Any female working in a male prison could not afford to be squeamish because she would be subjected to ruthless harassment, not only by the prisoners but also by her coworkers—an absolute, unshakable reminder of a double-edged sword. Therefore, to write a disciplinary report on every incident would not behoove me in the least bit. It was imperative that I learned how to handle situations with swift, stern, and immediate actions, instead of reactions, while demanding respect. Bear with me, but it is hard to discuss certain issues without going into detail and falling off track every now and then.

Let me go back to visits and closing time. It was obvious that when visits were coming to an end and the sex was brought to a screeching halt, some of the prisoners started behaving erratically as they prepared to return to their cells—but not before a rigorous, buck-naked body cavity search with face masks, flashlights, goggles, and gloves. It was mandatory that the prisoners remove every stitch of clothing as soon as they entered the search room. Only that chosen few went straight to their cellblocks after being allowed to lag behind to avoid the mandatory strip search. During this rigorous procedure, some prisoners would display a sense of urgency to get back to their cells for various reasons, such as dislodging deadly planted drugs. Certain prisoners were taken directly to the infirmary for a few reasons. One reason was because the prisoner was captured on the surveillance video stashing contraband in an undisclosed area of his body, and other reasons were due to their erratic behavior, nausea, and vomiting.

As soon as they stepped foot into the infirmary, they were obligated to undergo a prostate examination by a doctor. If the prisoner refused, he was hauled off to the hole, where he could possibly die from implanted or ingested lethal drugs. Otherwise, the doctor would insert his finger into the prisoner's rectum to seize any imbedded drugs. Usually this type of procedure is done exclusively for health purposes. In prison, it's done primarily for suspicion of smuggling of drugs and contraband. It was critical for other prisoners to get back to their cells expeditiously in order to induce a bowel movement and attempt to pass a drug packet, better known as an eight ball. This is a condom or plastic package filled with heroin, cocaine, or other drugs that they calculatedly swallowed attempting to bring into the prison. More than likely, that's what initiated the nausea rather than liquor intoxication. If they were unable to expel the eight ball in sufficient time, the packet could burst, releasing the lethal drugs into their bloodstream, and the prisoner would ultimately succumb to his death almost immediately. Sometimes, of course, the prisoners would reach their cells in enough time to remove the cleverly hidden contraband that was not seized during the search, whether the corrections officer overlooked it in error or on purpose.

These were some of the life-threatening reasons for their haste to get back to their cells. Countless prisoners have died in the process. It was mind-blowing what they would do for a quick fix.

Last, but not least, prisoners were in a hurry to get back to their cells hoping to take a cold shower to relieve themselves of the built-up semen they were unable to release during their erotic responses to their illicit sex.

The male corrections officers responsible for these exasperating bare-body searches were just as impatient to get through the annoying process. They had to put up with the prisoners' naked clammy skin and the pungent odor of poor hygiene and grimy sex, coupled with an erect or limp penis, oozing with semen. The culmination of this task was inspecting the prisoner's rectum area. At this time, the prisoner had to bend over, spread his butt cheeks, and cough in order to expel any suspected drugs imbedded in his rectum or held between his buttocks. It was virtually impossible to avoid an occasional splash of feces that accidentally or purposely excreted during the process; hence, the reason for the face masks, goggles, and gloves. In their haste, some highly agitated officers consequently yielded unsuccessful searches, which in turn enabled illegal contraband to gain access into the prison.

I am convinced, without question, that the greater part of my bare-body searches of female prisoners were in vain as well. That also goes for the pat frisks and searches of the female visitors— and especially my efforts to crack down on sexual misconduct— because as soon as the female was cleared and allowed to enter the visit area, she'd run to the bathroom, remove her panties, and stash any contraband that wasn't seized, rendering the whole process a waste of time. The prisoners who were chosen by design to clean the bathrooms would go in and retrieve the stashed contraband planted in those hidden designated areas. A consensus deceitfully reached by the visitor, the prisoner, and sometimes the officer before, during, and after visits. Remember—these were some of those so-called privileged prisoners, who were allowed to engage in sex and deliberately looked over during mandatory strip searches.

The women's bathroom, where the majority of the contraband was seized, also was a reflection of a combination of things. Above and beyond the fact that it was a hideout for contraband, it was looked upon as a crime scene, where evidence from sexual and physical assaults, such as bloody clothes and panties, was uncovered. Also, it was a place of refuge for females after being raped or beaten. It was a place for little ones to run and hide from fear and abuse. It was merely a smaller cesspool of horrors as opposed to the prison itself. It was a place where a female visitor could express her defiant attitudes toward female corrections officers, or officers in general, and even the prisoners they were visiting. By this I mean obscenities were smeared on the walls with feces, blood, and sometimes a pen or marker, even though writing material was prohibited inside. They unquestionably made their sentiments known, by their actions and writings, that no matter what, they were going to do whatever they wanted to do and get away with it. This was evident from the shredded, torn, and bloody undergarments left behind—the tragic signs of a forceful rape, their subtle cries for help, or simply their cavalier attitudes of defiance. Their disregard for themselves and their children was unconscionable.

Additionally, the women's bathroom was littered with soiled diapers, disposable baby bottles reeking of liquor, bloody sanitary pads and tampons, and again, women's and children's clothing. All of these items were strewn everywhere—in the sinks, on the floor, and in the stalls, floating or packed in the toilets leaving them backed up or overflowing. It seemed as though they had no use for the huge trash bins located inside the bathrooms. The smell was almost too much to bear and was more like toxic vapors that spilled out into the visit area. No matter how many times I did my spot checks, I never caught them doing any of these spiteful acts.

It was unfortunate and a disgrace that the female corrections officers had to use the same bathroom. We did not have the pleasure of separate female bathrooms in the visit center, nor inside the main prison, for that matter. This was the only female restroom in the entire prison. The bathrooms inside the main prison were gender-neutral, and we were obligated to use the same bathrooms the prisoners used, depending on their location. It was another tremendously demeaning and distressing position in which we were placed. Speaking of which, someone, whether it was an officer or a prisoner, was intentionally putting small holes in some of the bathroom doors. Therefore, each time I went to the bathroom, I had to stuff the tiny holes with tissue paper before relieving myself. Needless to say, my complaints, along with those of the other female officers, were considered frivolous. And so we just did what we had to do.

VOWING NEVER TO RETURN

SPEAKING OF BATHROOMS, THERE WAS a time I noticed that a female visitor had been in a stall for an unusually long time. I left and came back a few times, and she was still there. I waited for the rest of the ladies to leave, and then I informed her that we were alone and suggested that she come out. She was taking her sweet time to open the stall door, so I was confident that I had finally caught one of the women doing something illegal. To the contrary, as she slowly began to open the door, I could see that she was sweating profusely and gasping for air. I recognized her right away as being one of the regular visitors who had been visiting for years. I started to go for help, but she stopped me and said, "I'm all right. I just need to calm down." "What's going on?" I asked.

She was visibly shaken as she slowly replied, "I'm ashamed to tell you this, but my husband keeps shoving his hand into my snatch, and then he shoves his fingers into my rectum as hard as possible. It's so painful, and I'm bleeding. I know it's wrong, and I hate it. I want him to stop! He refuses and starts thrusting even deeper and harder. The more I beg him to stop, the harder he pushes. So I just bite my lip and don't say anything." I asked her why she didn't tell one of the officers. Shamefully, she held her head down and whispered, "The thought of what he might do to me, terrifies me. Anyways, I love him. Honestly, I don't want to go back out there with him, and I don't want to come back here ever again! Please help me!"

Sadly enough, I would hear stories like this every other weekend, but for some reason, this one struck a chord with me. She really seemed to be at a crossroads. We both knew that if she did not return to the visit area, it would not only mean repercussions for her, but more than likely repercussions for me as well—especially if he knew that she was divulging his actions. We both had reservations as we quickly contemplated what to do next. In the meantime, her husband was losing his patience and solicited another female to check on her. I immediately ordered this other female to go back to her seat, advising her that the visitor was ill.

I found myself being sympathetic toward her. I had a gut feeling that she was a good-natured woman, merely caught up in the game. I had seen her so many times throughout the years visiting her husband. She was always pleasant and respectful. The majority of the female visitors were unpleasant and disrespectful. She was just another subservient wife and believed that she had no way out. I was painfully aware of the fact that she was a product of domestic abuse, another battered wife behind the wall. I explained to her that I would do whatever I could to handle the situation if she was sincere about wanting to get out of the environment altogether. After all, her husband was incarcerated for life.

Her reply was heart wrenching. "If you help me, I will never come back here again. Please, get me out of this hellhole. I just want out! I didn't shoot and kill anybody, he did! Why do I have to go down with him?" she cried. In that same breath she mumbled, "But he has no one else in his corner." She was shaking like a leaf and reluctant to go back out into the visit area, not even to say goodbye. She could not stand the sight of him, she professed.

Acting on my instincts and with a heavy heart, I took a chance and led her out of the visit area, informing a lieutenant and other officers along the way of the lie I had concocted, which was that she was extremely ill. I had to come up with something serious in order for her to exit the visit center and vacate the premises. I was obligated to proceed in that manner in accordance with the number one rule, which was "under no circumstances will a visitor be allowed to leave on their own accord, except for emergencies." All visitors were required to exit at the same time. Once they were locked inside, the visitors were prisoners, much like the corrections officers or anyone else who entered the abyss. After escorting her outside, she was extremely appreciative and vowed never to return.

Like I said, I'd heard that statement repeatedly. I can count on one hand how many really meant it and never came back. My intuition wanted me to believe that she would be true to her word. From there, I went back to the visit center praying that I had made the right decision. I personally went and spoke to her husband, whose only concern was whether or not she divulged his sadistic behavior. He didn't say those exact words, but there was unspoken tension between us. To relieve him of any suspicion, I continued with my concocted story, adding that I insisted she leave immediately because she was too ill to stay, adding to the lie, that she really had wanted to continue with her visit. I further rationalized that I felt it was in her best interest to leave right away and seek medical attention, since she was vomiting. Surprisingly, he thanked me for looking out for his wife and returned to his cellblock without a problem.

Honestly, I was expecting a hostile response. Nevertheless, I presumed that she might feel driven to return or even discuss with him what really occurred in the bathroom. Therefore, I did not put myself completely out on the front line by banning her from visits or writing a disciplinary report, charging him with aggravated sexual assault. When the dust cleared, I was grateful that she kept her word. Months later though, her husband approached me on the tier and thanked me again. This time he added, "She needed that," and kept walking. He didn't go into detail, and I didn't inquire. I was happy that he was happy, and apparently she was happy too.

Please allow me to point out that, that was a rare occurrence, and I took a big gamble that day. She was one of the very few that I never saw again, and her husband always gave me the utmost respect when I was assigned to work on his tier. He never had another visit from anyone else from that point on. Perhaps it had to be done in that manner. It could be that was the only way he could get her to stop coming. If truth be told, there were many prisoners who, in reality, did not want their significant others and loved ones visiting them in prison and becoming part of the dehumanizing effects of the institution. Oftentimes the women were gluttons for punishment and came back as soon as the prisoner would have them.

This brings me to another incident involving a young prostitute. On this brutal winter day, the temperatures were in the single digits, with high gusty winds. It was the type of cold that bites through your clothes and through your skin, right down to your bones. The officers were all dressed as if we were Eskimos.

Nevertheless, the icy temperatures didn't make a difference to the women who stood in those long lines, wrapped around the outside of the prison, and slept in their cars waiting for the gates of hell to open for a visit. One would think that free money was being given away. When I arrived for duty just before sunrise, they had already formed a line, and the parking lot was full. Normally, if you will recall, the officers had to case the lines to check the visitors for inappropriate dress attire and any other violations before they were permitted to register. Not this day, it was freezing outside. You would think that everyone would be dressed appropriately, if not overdressed. To this day, I do not know how the men, women, and especially the children could withstand those record-breaking temperatures. It was always an unbelievably incredible sight to see.

Just for your information, visits were only cancelled in a state of emergency, declared by the governor, and an emergency lockdown. The prisoners probably would have taken over the prison at the mere thought of cancelling visits. They constantly boasted about visits being their right.

On this particular day, when the gates of hell finally opened, the visitors began to move past the officer with the metal detector and walk through the scan machine. That's when I saw a young lady, whom I had only seen once before about a year earlier. At that time, she was underage and accompanied by a well-known prostitute. This older, well-seasoned prostitute was known for introducing young girls to the prisoners, who would in turn put the girl's name on his visit list to become one of his paid prostitutes. Well, since that short span of time, her whole appearance had totally changed from the first time I saw her. She went from looking like an undeveloped, innocent, and beautiful young girl to looking like a worn-out tramp in about a year's time. To tell you that on that cold, blustery, windy day, she was underdressed would be a gross understatement. The closer she got to me, the more I could not comprehend what I was seeing, or rather I just didn't want to believe it.

At first glance, I instantly noticed that she was not wearing a hat, scarf, or gloves. Furthermore, it was inconceivable to realize that she did not have on any stockings and was wearing a pair of open-toe shoes. To add to this shock wave, she was wearing a leather, high school football bomber jacket. The straw that broke the camel's back, though, came when I asked her to remove her jacket and walk through the scan machine. She could hardly keep her balance because she was trembling as much as the gusty winds were blowing. Reluctantly, she began to remove her jacket while giving me a pitiful look, like a child who had just got caught with their hand in the cookie jar. I felt completely helpless watching her struggle to take off the jacket that was stiff as ice, revealing nothing but a paper-thin summer dress. I was almost positive that she was bare-naked underneath, so her skin was completely exposed to the wintry elements, that were just hovering above zero degrees.

For a split second, I could not grasp what was happening. It was unimaginable. I would not have believed it if I had not seen her with my own eyes. Why, and how, could she come out barely dressed into the bitter cold and stand in a line for hours to visit a monster of a man that she didn't even know? There was nothing this man could offer her. I just wanted to understand her mind-set. Why? How could her frail little body withstand those icy temperatures? Where were her parents and the people who loved her? While I was going crazy out of my mind, my eyes began to swell with tears, as did hers. It took all the strength I had not to grab and hold her close to me, just to keep her warm and protect her from the vultures that awaited her inside. She was an innocent baby! She was somebody's daughter! I was flabbergasted.

While she became the brunt of ridicule for some of the

officers and visitors, I tried to figure out what to do with her. Should I allow her to go inside and visit the prisoner so she could be devoured? At least she would be warm. Or should I reject the visit and make her turn right back around, forcing her to go back out into the bitter cold? At that point, she would have to wait for the visitors' charter bus that was scheduled to return later that afternoon. In the interim, the prisoner was toasty warm inside, where the heat was on full blast, and his only concern was fulfilling his insatiable appetite for sex. And, when his visit was over, he would return to his warm and cozy cell as she braced herself for the brutal temperatures, barely dressed.

At that juncture, I asked one of my coworkers to take my post for a few minutes. I had to leave the area and fight back my tears, something I had done too many times before. Over and over, I witnessed in shame and heartbreak how the young ladies came back and forth into this place of extreme immorality and squalor, only to be used like a wet, dirty rag. My emotions ran equally high when I registered the young men and women brought into the prison to serve time. They would be handcuffed and chained together by the shackles placed around their small ankles like wild beasts or slaves. To serve half or the remainder of their lives locked away from society, never to return to the free world again—unless they were hauled out in a body bag to their grave. Like babies lost in the wilderness, these same young men and women would have that same innocuous posture, the one where they looked as though they had just been caught with their hand in a cookie jar. As quickly as I turned away from their innocent faces, I was duty bound to turn right back around and face their truths.

Anyway, I was still contemplating how to handle this young lady who was frozen stiff. I could not help the fact that my motherly instincts were kicking in, and I just wanted to cling to her so she would be warm. That's when I instructed her to wait in a warm room, where she could literally thaw out. The room was actually a holding area for violators until the local police picked them up. In this instance, I merely wanted to question her before I made a conscious decision regarding her visit. Once again, a feeling of both compassion and anger had me in a pickle. But I had to compose myself before I could do anything.

When I entered the room, she was curled up in the corner shivering like a lost puppy. My composure instantly left my body as a single teardrop fell from my eye like an icicle falling from a tree. My first question was "Why are you doing this to yourself?" At the same time, I was saying under my breath, "Who the hell am I to be asking her such a personal question? She's not my daughter!" Lacking self-control, I persisted. I could see that my questioning brought her to shame. It was clear that she was very uncomfortable with what she was doing. From the inception of this one-sided conversation, it was my intention to keep her warm and away from the vultures, even if it was only for a short time. The fact remained that she was inappropriately dressed and not wearing any underwear; her dress was that revealing. I still did not know what to do first. My main concern was making sure she stayed inside from the blustery winds. Therefore, I did the best I could within my authority to prolong her wait. Still making every effort to drag out her stay, I left her in the room so some other officers could reason with her. Afterward I went back in and posed the pressing question, "Are you wearing any underwear?" She laughed nervously and answered an unconcerned no.

At that point, I was under an obligation to officially reject her from visiting. She immediately broke down and began crying like the little girl she was. I am not sure what precipitated her tears. Was it because she did not want to go back out into the cold, or was it because she couldn't visit this vulture? Maybe she was afraid of him. Or was it because she was ashamed? I wasn't getting it.

I wanted to console her, but I probably would have received a written reprimand for unethical practices. Therefore, I just gave her some tissue.

Then, in a flash, she went from zero to one hundred expressing her contempt. Maybe she was having an emotional meltdown, or she was really melting from the freezing cold and coming to her senses. I didn't know what was going on, but I let her vent. Some officers were ready to throw her out. In her fit of anger, she sneered, "These rules are so stupid. And who do you think you are, trying to get in my business? You are not my mother!" I didn't respond. I couldn't get a word in edgewise anyway. Agitated, she yelled nonstop in her high-pitched voice. "Why am I visiting this asshole anyhow? I am so stupid! I don't belong in this place. Let me the fuck up out of here! Right now!"

I was in awe. What got my attention was that she referred to herself as being stupid and started questioning her actions. She kept on with her angry outbursts as she started stomping her way back out into the freezing cold and gusty winds, vowing never to return. At the same time, she brushed off the officers who were trying to help her, even to the extent of turning down the arranged taxi service they had in place for her. She continued to voice her ongoing contempt and disrespect. "I don't need y'all to do nothing for me! I got money! I'll get my own cab. Y'all ain't got to worry about me no more. I won't be comin' back to this dump ever again!" She continued to rant, "What was I thinking in the first place? I never wanted to come here in the beginning! I don't need him. I can get what he got on the streets!"

Hearing and listening to her confused statements compelled me to do everything in my power to stop her from visiting altogether, from banning her for her tantrum and for lying about her relationship to the prisoner—she said she was his niece—to her inappropriate dress attire. The DOC ignored all of the above and allowed her to return and visit him from that point on, every week (in between the rejections for her inappropriate dress attire), until he impregnated her. Seven or eight months into her pregnancy, he died from full-blown AIDS. Her baby was born with HIV and passed away shortly after birth. She continued to be preyed upon until her death from the same disease. Dejected, she willingly accepted the predators to snatch her human spirit and dissect her soul.

EVERYONE HAS A
STORY TO TELL:
SEVEN SHORT STORIES OF
THE FEMALE PRISONER

Irreversible Catastrophe

SHE HAD BEEN IN JUVENILE detention once or twice before. She was serving time for fighting and stabbing another girl over a boy. The stab-wound victim survived, but she was sentenced to five years for aggravated assault with a deadly weapon. She was barely eighteen years old when she was convicted and transported to state prison. Now twenty-one years old, she had served three years of her five-year sentence when she verbally threatened a corrections officer for offending her with his sexual overtones. Her penalty was thirty days in the hole. (Let me point out that the hole in the females' prison was quite different from the hole in the males' prison. It was so different that I elected to go on duty there as a permanent post. Simply, it was quiet, clean, and secluded, and it housed less than fifty prisoners.)

As soon as she was housed in the hole, she would sing songs and recite poems while her cellmates, and I had no other choice but to listen. We didn't mind being her audience because she was that good. When she grew tired, she would thank us for listening, especially me, because I didn't tell her to "shut up" as she claimed other officers ordered her to do. She sang beautifully, her poems were intriguing, and she always seemed to be full of joy. I could not understand why such a talented young lady was locked away from the world, even though she had made a big mistake.

One night she was not her usual talkative self. All she had to say was "I've had enough. I can't do this anymore." Her fellow inmates and I tried our best to raise her spirits to no avail. That night, her audience did all of the talking. From down in the hole they were yelling from their dark cells, "Sing, girl! We want to hear you sing! Do some poetry. Come on, talk or something! We want to hear your voice!" In a low-pitched voice, she answered, "I can't, guys. I don't have it in me tonight."

At the end of my shift, she pleaded with me to stay a little longer. It was no problem for me, so I sat and conversed with her for a while through the small cubbyhole in the steel door that separated us. The time came when I had to go home to get some rest, so I could get back to work on time the next day. I said to her, "We'll talk tomorrow." Furthermore, my fellow officers did not take kindly to the attention I was giving her because she had verbally threatened a male officer. I informed the officer who relieved me of what I considered a dire situation. I did the same throughout the day, informing the senior officers and the medical staff. I explained that I deemed it necessary to have her placed on a supervised twenty-four-hour suicide watch because of her extreme mood change. She was awfully depressed.

This necessitated an additional officer to do one thing, and that was to sit and monitor her for the next twenty-four hours, while the other officer handled the other few prisoners who were in solitary confinement. However, the suicide watch had to be authorized by one of the senior officers. I was assured that they would follow through and place an additional officer on the overnight shift to watch her after I went home. Before I left she said to me, "Thanks for listening, but I won't be here tomorrow when you come in." I said, "I know, tomorrow is your thirtieth day, and you will be going back to your wing. Please do not allow them to pull you out of your character, forcing you here in the hole again. Do not let these male officers get into your head. If you're transferred back before I come in, I will come over to your wing and check you out." She slightly nodded her head in agreement and whispered, "Okay, I'll see you on the other side then." I said, "Okay."

When I returned for duty the next day, she had already been moved. To my horror, she'd been moved to a morgue in a nearby hospital. She really had gone to "the other side." She'd committed suicide by hanging herself in the middle of the night. This proved that she was never placed on the twenty-four-hour suicide watch. And besides that, the shift officer on duty had fallen asleep. He was reprimanded, but she was dead. They intentionally ignored her because she had verbally threatened a male officer, who was trying to get into her panties. Let me rephrase that: she refused to fuck a male officer.

This was just one of the horrific incidences in the female correctional facility. The verbal threats and sexual advances seeped in from both sides of the prison bars. She could not withstand the pressure—the pressure of long-term confinement, sexual advances, and the ultimatums that came with them. Which are, "If you suck me or fuck me, I won't write you up." I was devastated! I could not understand why some of the male officers allowed their penises to influence what they were obligated to do, especially when it came to the life of another human being.

Words cannot express the level of pain I felt in my heart that day. It was difficult to keep an emotional distance in not to become attached in these instances. I feigned illness and requested to go home that day. On my one-hour commute home, I wept as if she was my own daughter. I really did not want to believe that she fully intended to go through with such a senseless act. Most of all, I trusted that my fellow officers would do their duty and monitor her that night, in order to prevent an irreversible catastrophe. It was such a tragic and painful outcome of what I considered to be trust on life support.

❧ • WHY WAS GRANDMA IN JAIL?

I never really came right out and asked an inmate why he or she was incarcerated. I didn't have to, for the most part, because their convictions were what they talked about all day, every day. Whether they were remorseful about their mishaps or mistakes, bragging or boasting about wreaking havoc in their neighborhoods, or just pretending or embellishing to seek attention or to ward off other prisoners, it was everyday prison talk. Eventually, everyone would know why he or she was incarcerated.

One prisoner really aroused my curiosity. I had not heard anything about her conviction. She surely did not look like she belonged in a maximum security prison serving time. Actually, the way she carried herself reminded me of my grandmother. The color of her hair was pure silver, and she was about four feet eight inches tall. She moved about like a little butterfly as she assisted the other prisoners with their duties. Everyone seemed to cater to her. It appeared that she was revered a great deal among the inmates and the officers. You could see that she carried herself with great pride and dignity. After all, she was a mere eighty-eight years old. I was itching to find out what type of crime had placed her behind the bars of a state prison, where she appeared to be quite relaxed. Maybe she was convicted of a terrible crime when she was much younger and sentenced to a long prison term. Plainly, I wanted to know, why was Grandma in jail?

I was going to ask the other officers, but I wanted her to tell me. I really didn't want to pry until my curiosity got the best of me. I just came right out and asked her, "If you don't mind me prying, why are you here?" She replied gladly, "No, I don't mind; I don't mind at all. I have been here going on two years." Stunned, I shouted, "What? Two years?" Now if she had said thirty years, perhaps I could have identified with that a little better. But two years? Probing deeper, I asked, "But why?" She looked at me, laughed, and replied, "It's all right, sweetheart. I'm all right. I'm comfortable, and I feel safe here. I get a lot of love and respect. I get three decent meals, I have friends I can talk to, and most of all I can sleep at night. I look forward to dying here. At least I'll be at peace."

While I listened with fixed attention, as I would listen to my own grandmother, she continued, "The reason that I am here is because my grandson is a drug dealer. He and his friends use my home to sell drugs to those people in the streets. The police broke into my home so many times that I lost count. Every time they came, my grandson was running the streets or hiding. Him and his friends smoked drugs and drank liquor, and the house was full of piss-tail girls. My home was filthy, and he never cleaned.

I couldn't sleep when he was there, and I couldn't sleep when he wasn't there. The last time the law kicked my door down, I begged them to take me away from my own home, the same home that I have loved and cherished for over fifty years. I told the lawman not to leave me alone. I was afraid they would make a mistake and shoot me, or kill my grandson right before my eyes. My grandson constantly disrespected me and refused to leave my home. I have fewer years in front of me than I do behind me, and I choose not to live them in fear. So I told the law officers that the drugs belonged to me, so take me away to the jailhouse. They knew better, but they had a job to do.

"I am very happy and content here. I never want to go back home again. This is my home now. All I can do is pray for my grandson. It's just a matter of time before he is killed or goes to the jailhouse. I don't worry anymore; I just pray. I'm just glad that I don't have to worry about the lawman breaking my door down anymore. I'm safer right here in the jailhouse." I was mesmerized, and I said to her, "Ma'am, thank you for sharing. What a tragic tale, but I do understand. God bless you."

JUST GIRLS DOING WHAT GIRLS DO

I wrote about the vast homosexuality in the female correctional facility and the confrontational attitudes I faced with some of the women, whether they were homosexual or heterosexual. In retrospect, looking at the big picture, I appreciated working with the females because we were one and the same, and we tended to have quite a few serious and heartfelt conversations. This is a very short and funny story about one of the female prisoners, who expressed her sentiments about being locked up.

I was working in a dorm house, which is an open sleeping quarters in the medium security section of the prison. I would say about thirty prisoners were housed in this dorm at the time. I was doing my last-minute rounds before my shift ended, and the ladies and I were having one of our usual conversations about life. Just as I was about to leave, out of the blue, one of the prisoners said to me, "Do you realize that I've been locked up for six years now, and I haven't had sex with a man since I've been here?" I said to myself, "Oh boy, where is she going with this one?"

Although she was addressing me, she was speaking loud enough that everyone in the dorm could hear her and were listening. I casually responded, "Really?" Then she came back with, "I am about to fuck one of these fine male officers in here!" I reacted right away. "Girrrrl, don't do it to yourself. You are about to approach the finish line! You are on your way out the door!" She threw up her hands in frustration and yelled out, "I am tired of this carpet-munching shit! I need some penetration!" Catching me and everyone else completely by surprise, we all burst into laughter. We must have laughed for a good five minutes.

I eventually said to her, "You'll be all right for one more year. Don't get yourself into any more trouble. Go home." Her response was "I just said that to make you laugh. I was thinking about it though. But I am not going to do anything else to jeopardize my chances of being away from my children again. For real though, I ain't with this carpet-munching shit. I can't wait to get out there and get with a man." Then she and the other prisoners said, "Good night, see you tomorrow." I responded with a smile. "Y'all be good; see you tomorrow."

I must say this was one of the nights that I went home feeling a sense of accomplishment as a corrections officer. I felt as though the prisoners respected me and appreciated the respect I had for them. It showed that it was possible to coexist in such an awkward environment, without the strife that prison life can bring. I was flattered that they did something not only to make me laugh, but also something that we could all laugh about together. I also recognized the fact that they trusted me enough to share their personal feelings as females, and for that moment, we were just girls doing what girls do.

🦋 • IT'S ALL MY FAULT

I was on my way to work and running late. I'm squirming in my seat as I say to you that I was driving over one hundred miles per hour in my brand-new Lexus, which was barely a month old. It was a miracle that I wasn't pulled over by the state troopers. I could have caused a serious accident, weaving in and out of traffic like I was crazy. The only thing I was thinking about was getting to lineup on time and avoiding a written reprimand from chief tits-tosterone, as we called her. She was looking for any reason to ruin my chances for a transfer.

My hustle and bustle—with my foot heavy on the pedal, putting everyone's life on the road in danger—didn't make a bit of difference because there was a car accident ahead of me that brought the traffic to a complete standstill. At this point, I had no other choice; I had to notify the prison that I was going to be late. Fortunately, several officers who were on the road ahead of me had already notified the prison of the accident. The traffic ended up stalled for over three hours. When the troopers finally cleared one lane for passing, everyone crept along to get a glimpse of the aftermath of the horrendous crash. It was a graphic scene, to say the least. I did not realize it was a fatal car accident until I saw one of the victims lying lifeless on the road, partially covered by a small blanket. It would have only taken a second to totally cover the body. "The indecency of it all," I said to myself. It was all too apparent that she was deceased. I assumed it was a woman when I got a glance of her fancy stockings and shoes. At that moment,

I felt a strong sense of compassion for her loved ones, who had no idea what was happening at that precise moment. From that point on, I could not get that picture out of my head for the rest of the day.

Finally, when I arrived for duty four hours into my shift with ten other stragglers, I was emotionally depleted, mainly from seeing that woman's lifeless body lying on the side of the road as if she was roadkill. My whole day was chaotic from the time I'd left home until my shift ended. At least I didn't receive a reprimand. Most of all, I was grateful that I didn't cause a fatal car accident when I reflected on how I was driving like a maniac at the same time.

When I relieved the officer who was standing post for me, she reminded me that one of the prisoners was waiting to be released to go home. Hearing that small piece of information cheered me up a little because that prisoner was a pleasant and mature young lady. She was incarcerated for writing some bad checks during hard times, as she put it. She seemed to have learned her lesson and set a positive example for the other young prisoners in the trailer. A trailer is a setup for prisoners with less than a year remaining to be released. It was located on the outside perimeters of this maximum security prison. It was completely unsecured by walls, gates, or fences. She was so excited about going home, and everyone appeared to be just as excited for her because she and her partner were going on a venture, to find a place that recognized same-sex marriage. Comradery, was not usually shared among many of the prisoners when one was about to go home. The atmosphere surrounding those who were about to be released usually was rife with jealousy and envy. On occasion, this would precipitate a conflict and a physical altercation. However, she seemed to be on an even keel with everyone.

When she came out into the open area prepared to leave, I

was so tensed about what I had seen and gone through earlier that I almost forgot that she was going home. I said to her, "You should have been gone by now. What's the holdup?" She gleefully responded, "I know, my wifey-to-be is running a little late." I said, "She must be caught up in the same traffic jam that caused me to be late for work today."

While we waited for her to be escorted to the front gate, without thinking, I proceeded to tell her and the other prisoners about the horrific car crash. I pointed out how the troopers allowed one of the victims to be partially covered, exposing the bottom half of a body. Just then I received a call from the command station, informing me that an officer was enroute to escort the prisoner to the gate for her release. Her fellow inmates gave her a hug and so did I, against policies and procedures. "So what?" I said to myself. "She's going home." We all wished her well. Then I stressed to her, "I don't want to see you back here again!" She just looked at me, smiled, and said, "Girrrl, I'm outta here. I'm gettin' married," and proceeded to leave with the officer. One of the prisoners yelled out, "Don't forget about us, and don't forget to write either. Send us some pictures too!" Excitedly she replied, "I won't, and I will definitely send y'all some pictures!" From that joyous moment on, I figured the remainder of my short workday was going to be much better.

I was about an hour into my work routine when I suddenly saw her running back toward the trailer. For obvious reasons, running on the grounds of a prison was a serious violation. Despite that, she was frantically running ahead of the officer who was supposed to be escorting her. He didn't seem moved by her actions, nor did the other officers in the surrounding area. That's when I started to realize something out of the ordinary was happening. As she got closer, I could hear her calling my name. I thought that the front command station had made a mistake on her release date, or she found out that she had additional charges, or another county had a warrant for her to be picked up. Therefore, they put a hold on her release. This would not have been the first time that something like this has happened, although I hadn't received a call concerning anything. No matter what, nothing could have prepared me for what happened next.

When she finally reached the trailer, she was so distraught and out of breath that she could barely speak. I was trying my best to calm her down and stop her from hyperventilating, so she could speak clearly enough that I could understand her. But, she was inconsolable. The officer who was escorting her came strolling in minutes behind her and stared at us in awe, instead of explaining the matter at hand. Perhaps he was in awe because I was comforting a prisoner. Then again, I didn't care. I continued to comfort her, as did the female prisoners, especially since she was squeezing the breath out of me while uncontrollably quivering and crying. "Don't just stand there looking stupid!" I shouted to the escorting officer. "What in the world is going on? How much longer does she have to stay? What's her new release date?"

Without warning, she interjected with a loud, piercing cry, "My wife is dead! My wife is dead! My wife is dead! She was killed in that car accident on her way here to pick me up. That was my wife that you saw lying on the ground dead!" Distraught, she kept crying out, and I held her even tighter. "It's all my fault. It's all my fault. If I wasn't in jail, she wouldn't have been on that highway on her way here to pick me up. She would be alive! It's all my fault!" she said repeatedly. She uttered that heartbreaking statement again and again, until she was eventually taken to the infirmary where she was sedated, and her babbling gave way to sleep. Needless to say, I was overwhelmed and rendered speechless. Crushed with grief, she'd rather remain incarcerated than go home, knowing, the tragedy she had to face.

🦋 • A REAL WHODUNIT

My shift was ending, and I could not wait to get home. I had been working in the tower that day, so I was heading toward the arsenal to relinquish my weapons and get out of there. Suddenly I heard the loud wailing of the emergency siren. This meant the prison was preparing for an emergency lockdown. Subsequently, all officers are automatically obligated to remain behind the wall indefinitely. There were no exceptions to this rule, even if the officer had already clocked out as I had. This lockdown was strangely different because no one was informed about the urgency of the matter. We were just ordered to return to the lineup room, where we were given special assignments and instructed to remain on post until further notice. This procedure was exceptionally peculiar because the officers were usually informed immediately of an issue; it only made sense. This time we were left to wonder as the night wore on.

Every time I looked up at the clock, seemingly every other minute, it was as though the hands were not moving. I vividly remember looking at the clock when it was 1:30 a.m. The last time I was out on the grounds was at 10:00 p.m., and I thought I was on my way home. I could not believe that we had not received any information concerning the urgency for a lockdown, not even the slightest hint. I felt like a sitting duck. The entire institution seemed to be asleep, including the officer who was on post with me. Apart from the fact that neither of us was supposed to be sleeping, we agreed to take turns. I wanted to go to sleep first, but my anger would not allow me to. All I could think about was my long drive home and wonder why we were being kept in the dark about something as serious as a lockdown in a maximum security prison.

Then, out of nowhere, I saw flashing lights and some

movement outside. An array of officers and a female prisoner were walking toward the Internal Affairs Office (IAO). Soon thereafter, the predawn light made it visible enough to see exactly who it was as they exited the building. It was the newly appointed chief, the captain, a sergeant, and two officers from IAO with the same prisoner, but this time she was handcuffed and shackled. It now was going on eight hours since the official lockdown. For me it was going on sixteen hours; others had been there for almost twenty-four hours, and no one knew a thing. At least no one was saying anything. It wasn't like we weren't calling each other throughout the night, attempting to find out who knew what.

Eventually the first shift started strolling in, only to be locked down with everyone else. Even though first shift was arriving, no one could leave the prison. The prison remained on lockdown for several more hours, and we were still clueless. We thought we had a breakthrough when the chief began to make an announcement. However, we were under a false impression; he just wanted us to get the prisoners ready for questioning. He stated, "IAO will be coming to certain units to question certain prisoners, so be prepared."

Before I could turn around, the IA officers were walking into the unit. Just as my partner and I were about to round up the prisoners for questioning, one of the IA officers said, "There's no need for that. We are not going to ask them any questions; we are here to question you, both of you." The other officer and I said almost simultaneously, "The captain stated that the prisoners were going to be questioned." Again, before I could blink an eye, one of the IA officers started questioning us. "Do you know who this prisoner is?" Meanwhile, he's flashing her inmate ID photo at us. We both replied at the same time, "Yes." Then he hit us with, "Did you know she's pregnant?" Taken aback, I reacted right away. "Pregnant? How could she be pregnant?" The IA officer responded, "That's why we are here. This is what we want to know!" Without taking a breath, he continued, "She has been incarcerated for fifteen years of her two life sentences for murdering her husband and her boyfriend." Once again, I quickly responded, "That's no secret."

My partner was cool as a cucumber and simply stated, "Pregnant, wow." I was like a fish out of water and could not keep my mouth shut. "Oh my God! You mean to tell me that this is the reason the prison is on a lockdown? Because of a pregnant prisoner?" The IA officer alleged, "We don't know what's going on. For all we know there may be a perpetrator living on the premises." Then he posed another question: "So you've never noticed her weight gain or perhaps an officer that she might be smitten with?" We both answered no. I could not understand their antagonistic approach or their questions about a sexual affair. And I didn't want to fan the flames by adding more tension to what was already in the air, so, at that point I stopped overreacting and kept my thoughts to myself. Apparently, my partner caught that drift from the door, because he did not have too much to say from the onset.

It was obvious that they were trying to get some inside information from the officers. I really believed that if they wanted accurate answers, they would have questioned the prisoners. The prison was *their* world, and they knew the answers to everything that was going on. After the IA officers left, my partner and I just looked at each other perplexed. "Why are they interrogating the officers?" I said out of curiosity. He agreed, "Yeah," he said, "I was thinking the same thing. I don't understand that either." Be that as it may, before they came in to interrogate us, I had been complaining all night long about wanting to go home. Now I had this burning desire to stay and find out the answer to this mysterious quest. It had to be a corrections officer, or some other male employee, who impregnated the beautiful female prisoner. I was all eyes and ears. You could not pay me to go home at that point. We are talking about a real whodunit here! The notion about a perpetrator on the premises was a bunch of you-know-what. They knew something and wanted to see who knew what.

Not long after that, the prison lifted the lockdown, and I clocked out at around nine o'clock that next morning. After being awake all night long, I flew home, freshened up, and drove right back to the prison, forgetting all about sleep. One thing I knew for sure, when I got back to the prison, the mystery would be solved. Somebody knew something. It was strange, though, because I'd heard nothing as scandalous as a beautiful convicted murderess— who was incarcerated for fifteen years and never received a visit— was six months pregnant. This was a tale straight out of a mystery novel. Everyone seemed to be just as inquisitive as I was. If that was not a topic for discussion, I don't know what was.

When I arrived for duty, everyone was buzzing around like busy little bees flying all over the place with inquisitive looks on their faces. We all were waiting to hear who knew what. But that didn't happen. The captain proceeded with the usual call for lineup and delegated our regular assignments. The next chain of events was like a scene from a dramatic movie clip.

We were all gathering for lineup when two detectives from the county prosecutor's office walked into the room with the same two IA officers who had questioned us earlier that morning. Walking behind them were the state commissioner, the chief, and the handcuffed pregnant prisoner. While they stood with the prisoner, the detectives and the IA officials walked aggressively toward the captain, who was delegating the assignments at the time. They demanded that he turn around and place his hands behind his back. He stopped talking and just stood there looking at them. Without reiterating, they forcibly handcuffed him. To the astonishment of everyone watching and listening, the captain was the only person speaking as they promptly guided him out the door into a waiting unmarked police vehicle. He was in an uproar, yelling and screaming, "This is bullshit! I would never stoop so low as to have sex with a prisoner without a condom!"

That's when it hit everyone. It was the captain! The captain did it! He continued yelling, proclaiming his innocence. He even went as far as to say, "Me? Have unprotected sex with a filthy prisoner? What type of fool would do that? She's a fuckin' ingrate! I was trying to fulfill her needs! This is what I get in return? I have a pregnant wife at home! I don't need her!" He went on and on. My mouth was jarred open as I watched what was happening right before my eyes. The captain adamantly denied his involvement with her until she gave birth and DNA testing proved that he had fathered her baby girl. Meanwhile, he was married, and his wife was expecting their first child, which he had been boasting about for weeks.

The culmination of the sad circumstances surrounding this story is that his wife miscarried and lost their baby girl shortly after hearing the startling news about his infidelity and impending imprisonment. The captain was sentenced to a lengthy term in an out-of-state prison for malfeasance in office, sodomy, aggravated sexual assault, and terroristic threats—threatening to kill her if she revealed their sexual involvement.

FROZEN

This male officer worked first shift, and I was on second shift. We had the same days off and were assigned to the same post. We came in contact with one another every day during shift change. He was an exceptionally narrow-minded human being. He personified male chauvinism and sexism. Each day when I arrived for duty to make the shift change, he couldn't just hand me the keys and go over the usual breakdown of the day; he would take another five to ten minutes mulling over his list of write-ups he had accumulated throughout his shift. In doing so, I was compelled to request on several occasions that he refrain from referring to the female inmates as "bitches." It was a degrading term toward women, thereby showing lack of respect for me as well.

Like so many law enforcement officers, he had this enormous sense of empowerment and would revoke the prisoners' privileges constantly, not for a cause but just because he could. This was another open dorm area where the females could roam around somewhat freely. Due to his egotistical, authoritative measures, they were losing time in the yard, in the game area, on the phones, and watching television for no apparent reasons. He was imposing trivial sanctions for three, four and sometimes eight days at a time, strangely, falling short of having them remanded to the hole. I say strangely because ten days or more constituted a prisoner being remanded to the hole, pending an investigation. I was baffled because he appeared to be harassing the same set of females on a regular basis. If they were that unruly, why not remand them to the hole for further discipline?

I couldn't understand what was going on; neither could the other officers who worked the unit. Some of his petty penalties were because "her bed wasn't made" or "she didn't clean the bathroom good enough." His favorite one was "she was unbecomingly dressed." I started noticing that there was one certain female who was always on his hit list. I never had a problem with her, nor did any other officer.

Fed up with his pettiness and abuse of authority, I was tempted to write him up on his work ethic. I asked him quite a few times, "What's up with you and the petty sanctions every single day?

You are the only officer that has a problem on this unit." In his contemptuous manner, he responded, "They are all a bunch of low-life bitches, and they are always giving me back lip when I order them to do something, namely that one." He was giving that particular female a death stare. "She has a slick tongue. Every time I order her to do something, she has something to say."

By this time, I was fuming. His disposition was totally unacceptable. I yelled out, "First of all, you and the *bitch* word are out of control!" It was evident, that my words went right over his head because he kept popping his chops. "They act like tramps, so I treat them like tramps." I was so pissed off that I had to take a deep breath and remember where I was because I was about to curse this fool out. So, on that note, I quickly checked myself and decided it was time for me to step back from the situation since I was getting ready to put myself in a precarious position. I figured I would fall back a little and let him handle things his way, and I would continue to handle things my way. It was only a matter of time before he would be ousted from the unit. At least, that's what I was hoping. He was constantly having a heated war of words with everyone. Shockingly, before leaving the unit that day, he said, "Okay, I'll chill on the *B* word for you."

I was pretty sure that the supervisors knew of his chauvinistic ways and were just ignoring it, allowing him to carry on. The situation was out of control and out of my hands. In his eyes, and the eyes of some of the other male officers, I was just another bitch. At least most of the prisoners would get a break every now and then, but he was always having problems with that one young female prisoner. She'd usually be confined to her bed and, get this, not allowed to speak to the other prisoners on his watch. Where in the world did he get that from? He had her sit on her bed with her face turned toward the wall, and he was adamant about the other prisoners not speaking to her, or else, according to him, they would be admonished. He was abusing his authority to the limit. He was devising his own rules. Having her turn her face toward the wall? Really? Like small children, the other prisoners would rush to me as soon as he left the unit to get permission to speak to her. Under no terms was I about to follow through with any of his unreasonable restrictions.

I questioned her and the other prisoners on various occasions. "What in the world is going on? What is the problem?" The whole situation was absurd. They would shrug it off by replying, "He's just mean and doesn't like women, especially her." I knew there was more to it than that, but I could not put my finger on it. All I knew was that he was a nasty son of a biscuit eater, and I was on the verge of saying something to this joker that I knew I would regret. I could only imagine how he was treating her and the rest of the prisoners during a full eight-hour shift. When he came around, they would scatter like ants.

One afternoon when I came on duty, the young prisoner was once again confined to her bed. This jerk could not leave fast enough before a few of the ladies ran up to me and asked if she could get out of bed because she wanted to talk to me. It turned out that they all wanted to talk. There was no way I was going to condone his demeaning treatment when I had control of the unit. Occasionally I would think about another prisoner letting the cat-out-of-the-bag, but that was something I dealt with daily, all in accordance with my theory of trust on life support. Therefore, I told them to tell her to come to the front desk.

They all gathered around my desk like children with her standing in the middle. Before she opened her mouth, I asked her, "Why are you always getting into so much trouble with this guy? Sooner or later, he is going to have you remanded to the hole, and you know what that means regarding your release date. Whatever you are doing to set him off, you need to stop." While

I was talking to her, huge crocodile tears started rolling down her cheeks, and she immediately covered her face with her sweater. One of the other prisoners pulled her hands away from her face and shouted, "Don't be ashamed. Hold your head up, and tell the officer what he's doing to you, girl!"

She slowly raised her head and angrily said, "Every morning when that mutherfucka comes in here, he comes to my bunk and makes me get out of bed and clean the bathrooms. Then he comes to whichever bathroom I'm cleanin' and forces me down on my knees. Then he pulls out his dick and mushes it all over my face, pushes my head down, and makes me suck him off. After that he writes up those bogus, fucked-up reports and threatens to put me back in maximum if I tell anyone, especially you. All the girls in the unit already know." While they were all nodding their heads in agreement, she carried on. "If I go to the hole, I'm done; it's over. Nobody is going to believe my story. I wanna get the fuck up outta here! So, I do what he tells me to do. My time is limited in this mofo! I want to go home!"

Astonished, I paused and said, "You can't be telling me the truth! Why are you talking now?" Then they all started speaking at the same time. "We knew that nobody would believe her, so we set his ass up." I'm like, "OMG! What are you talking about? I'm not getting it!" Then the prisoner said, "He did it again this morning!" Again, I yelled out, "Oh my God! You guys are stressing me out with this garbage. I don't believe this mess! What do you expect me to do? You know you need proof!" She pleaded, "Please listen to me, please! That mutherfucka shot off another load of his hot, slimy wax into my mouth and, as usual, told me to swallow it! He says to me every single time, 'It's good for you, baby girl. You'll live longer.' This time," she said, "I pretended that I swallowed it, but instead I held it in my mouth. One of the girls purposely distracted him so he forgot to check in my mouth this time, and I spit that poisonous shit into a plastic baggie as fast as I could. Then another girl put it in the freezer with her name on it."

Once again, I screamed out in total disbelief, "What? I don't believe y'all! I don't believe it!" Without skipping a beat, she screamed back at me, "For real, Officer, I'm telling you the truth. That poisonous shit is in a plastic bag, in the freezer right now!" Dazed, I replied, "At this very moment?" Victoriously, she shouted, "Yes! I swear to you!" I didn't know whether to jump for joy in celebration of womanhood, give them all a standing ovation for such a brilliant idea, or shake my head in shame and disgust. Undoubtedly, I knew something was wrong, but never would I have imagined in my wildest dreams that he was sexually abusing a scumbag bitch, according to his description. According to him, they were "low-life tramp bitches, scums of the earth." His audacity astounded me. Moreover, when one of the prisoners retrieved the plastic baggie containing his semen from the freezer, you could stick a fork in me; I was done.

Now everything was coming full circle with respect to his outlandish disposition. I still could not take it all in as truth, even after I placed the frozen substance into an evidence bag, sealed it and signed it, all in the presence of an Internal Affairs officer. I have to say, I was still a little skeptical. No, I was a lot skeptical, period! There was no way he could be that asinine! I must say, gloatingly, that I was wrong. A serious investigation was launched, and the test proved he was more than asinine; he was a sex offender, a pedophile, and a criminal. Inevitably, he was arrested and convicted of aggravated rape, malfeasance, blackmail, and the list goes on. He was confined to a state prison where he remained in solitary confinement because of his violent behavior toward the corrections officers. Just so you'll know, his utterly ridiculous defense was that the "dirty bitch" in his words, watched him ejaculate in the female prisoner's bathroom, and when he left, she went behind him, licked up the semen off the floor, and put it in the plastic bag simply to frame him. Hearing about his preposterous testimony brought me back to one of the last conversations he and I had about her, in which he said, "She has a slick tongue," referring to her talking back to him. In retrospect, I found his choice of words hilarious. Unbelievably, some of my peers, men and women, were opposed to how I handled the situation. They had the audacity to suggest that I should have discarded the evidence against a sexually crazed predator simply because he was a corrections officer.

🦋 • KNEES DON'T HAVE FINGERS.

I lost count of how many times we had to forcibly strap her into a restraint chair, with a muzzle wrapped around her entire head, and tape her mouth to prevent her from spitting and biting the officers. She continued to make senseless attempts to go on with her usual combative behavior, but this time it was in a lethargic state because she was heavily sedated and confined to the infirmary's psychiatric ward. This particular rampage was beyond her usual range because she was not permitted to visit her husband, who was also incarcerated. It wasn't as if she had ever visited him before. She was psychotic and wanted to blame her daughter for the criminal behavior of her husband and her. "My daughter, who is a fuckin' slut and a fuckin' liar, is the reason I can't see my husband."

In her uncontrollable rages, she would scream and shout nonstop. "My daughter desperately needs her ass kicked, and when I get out of here, I'm going to be the one to do it. I should have killed her a long time ago. I tell you what, I am going to kill her when I get home, especially for what she's putting my man through!" Her uncontrollable, violent behavior and constant outbursts had a continuous pattern. She was extremely contentious and constantly in and out of the psychiatric medical wing and solitary confinement. She was an absolute headache for the officers and medics on a daily basis. She was definitely one of the many prisoners who needed to be committed to an insane asylum. From her cell port, she would spit and throw her feces and urine. No matter how many days she was remanded to the hole, it was apparent that she was simply incorrigible.

Eventually she was sentenced to spend the remainder of her thirty-year sentence in an enforced isolation unit. There she would remain on lockdown the entire time. The only time she left her cell—handcuffed and shackled, escorted by armed officers—was to go to a shower cellblock, where they hosed her down since she refused to shower on her own. She was incarcerated for aggravated criminal sexual abuse, sodomy of a child, endangering the welfare of a child, terroristic threats, possession of a controlled dangerous substance, and possession of multiple illegal firearms. She set out to be on an even greater warpath that day because she was informed that her pedophiliac husband was being transported to an out-of-state prison exclusively for sex offenders and their heinous sex crimes.

Prior to her incarceration, she tried to coerce her six-year-old daughter into lying about her father's sexual abuse. Yes, this is the daughter she was referring to. In her pathetic attempts to convince the court to believe her preposterous story, she admitted that she was aware of the fact that her husband was sexually abusing their daughter. Yet, she still attempted to explain, the unexplainable, by asserting, "So what? My husband made an honest mistake. It was only a few times. He told me exactly what happened. He actually thought she was me because she was so fuckin' fat. She should have let him know, but she wanted him to fuck her. She wanted it. She wanted him. It was just his knee that brushed up against her a couple of times. It was just his knee!" She continued with her madness. "My husband told me that she was lying, and I believe my husband. He told me that our daughter wanted to have sex with him. How could you believe a child over her parents? She's a fuckin' whore and a liar! He warned me that this was going to happen."

In spite of this sickening story and the nauseating circumstances surrounding it, what stood out most to me was one piece of information that they tried to persuade the child to believe: that it was his knee that rubbed up against her private area. On the face of it all, the six-year-old child was the wiser one and had to inform the adults who did not quite understand. She put it in plain and simple terms when she said, "Knees don't have fingers."

🦋 • THE RIGHT TO BEAR ARMS VS. ARMED AND DANGEROUS

As soon as I completed my one year of probation, which was required in order for me to carry a personal firearm, I immediately went out and bought a Glock .357 Magnum automatic pistol. It was one of the approved off-duty weapons, according to the firearms instructor, who worked with me tirelessly on the range. He explained that this particular firearm would be more suitable for me because it was a smaller weapon and easier to handle. After that first year of chaos and uncertainty as a rookie, I deemed it imperative to carry an off-duty weapon. It didn't take long for me to retract that statement. It was a completely different ball game carrying my own personal gun outside of the prison—in my car, in my home, and in public around innocent people. It was an especially strange feeling having a loaded gun in the presence of my children. Self-doubt made me feel like everyone around me was at risk, including myself. My initial reason for purchasing a weapon was my concern about parolees retaliating outside on the streets. Be that as it may, what also crept up in my thoughts was the potential that one of my children could accidentally get killed by having a gun in the house—even when I took into account that I purchased it for our protection. We hear about accidental shootings all the time.

Once I had the free will to carry it in public, I no longer felt safe. I know—it sounds confusing, right? I could not bond with the weapon like I did when I was in uniform and inside the prison. My awareness of the alarming number of deaths, by murder and suicide, at the hands of corrections officers brandishing their personal firearms outweighed my fear of retaliation from a parolee. I became acutely aware that certain people who owned a gun had the tendency to behave in a certain way, whether they were an officer, on or off duty, or a civilian with a license to carry. Some gun owners had the propensity to use their weapons at the drop of a hat. This irresponsible behavior had caused scores of fatalities merely because the gun owner was reckless and criminally negligent.

I did not want to become one of those careless statistics. To tell you the truth, I started becoming so panicky that I would leave my weapon in the arsenal inside the prison more often than having it on my person. Now what sense did that make? I had reached a point where I did not even want to see it or touch it. Nor did I want to have the weapon in my home, even though it was safely locked away. Moreover, that eventually turned out to be preposterous to me as well. Safely locked away? What does that mean? Guns are not safe! In addition to that thought, I believe that if you own a gun, it should be on your person or in your reach at all times. Otherwise, what is the sense of having it?

I worked myself into a state of paranoia. I had to get rid of it. I contemplated selling it to another officer. However, on the flip side, I did not want the gun that I sold to someone turn up in yet another murder or suicide, committed by a corrections officer. In the end, I decided to sell it back to the manufacturer. It's been said that "guns don't kill people ... people kill people." Here is my opinion with respect to that statement:

During target practice, while in the academy, and subsequently qualifying every six months on the range, we were taught to "shoot to kill." During shooting practice, the goal was to aim for the head and heart areas on the target and then shoot; that was the key to accuracy and the key to a perfect score. This was contrary to the department's claim that we were taught to "shoot to stop." I would guess that you are saying to yourself, "Then why did you remain on the job?" My answer to that is simple: money and health care benefits. I did not aspire to become a corrections officer, and I believe that rings true with most individuals who apply for the job.

There are people I know personally who work harder than I could ever imagine and do not have health care coverage. Therefore, I am sincerely grateful to have had a job with an exceptional health care plan. It was the salary and the health benefits that kept me from walking off the job many a day. I cannot tell you how many times I wanted to abandon my post and never look back. With all due respect, I equate the scenario of taking the position of a corrections officer—only to a minuscule degree—to the countless number of young men and women who enlist in the US Armed Forces. A good number of them do so because of the job security, health benefits, and education. It is not always because they want to go into combat. Either way, I thank God for their service.

This is a harsh truth. Financing a decent education, career, and health benefits is a serious uphill battle in America. Consequently, young people do the next best thing and join the service or take on a secure job that will support them and their families. Unequivocally, I say this, though: there is nothing in this world compared to the bravery and courage that it takes to go into combat. People do what is necessary to survive in this world and keep their families afloat. Therefore, to that end, it was well worth undertaking employment in the Department of Corrections, notwithstanding the fact that it was an absolute nightmare and a true expression of Trust on Life Support.

Printed in the United States
By Bookmasters